AF278386

Alabaster

by Audrey Cefaly

Winner of the 2017 David Calicchio Emerging American Playwright
Prize at Marin Theatre Company, Mill Valley, CA
Jasson Minadakis, Artistic Director | Keri Kellerman, Managing Director

FOR ENGLISH-LANGUAGE PRODUCTION INQUIRIES

UNITED STATES AND CANADA
info@concordtheatricals.com
1-866-979-0447

UNITED KINGDOM AND EUROPE
licensing@concordtheatricals.co.uk
020-7054-7298

Each title is subject to availability from Concord Theatricals Corp., depending upon country of performance. Please be aware that *ALABASTER* may not be licensed by Concord Theatricals Corp. in your territory. Professional and amateur producers should contact the nearest Concord Theatricals Corp. office or licensing partner to verify availability.

For all enquiries regarding motion picture, television, and other media rights, please contact Gurman Agency LLC, www.gurmanagency.com.

MUSIC AND THIRD-PARTY MATERIALS USE NOTE

Licensees are solely responsible for obtaining formal written permission from copyright owners to use copyrighted music and/or other copyrighted third-party materials (e.g., artworks, logos) in the performance of this play and are strongly cautioned to do so. If no such permission is obtained by the licensee, then the licensee must use only original music and materials that the licensee owns and controls. Licensees are solely responsible and liable for clearances of all third-party copyrighted materials, including without limitation music, and shall indemnify the copyright owners of the play(s) and their licensing agent, Concord Theatricals Corp., against any costs, expenses, losses and liabilities arising from the use of such copyrighted third-party materials by licensees. For music, please contact the appropriate music licensing authority in your territory for the rights to any incidental music.

IMPORTANT BILLING AND CREDIT REQUIREMENTS

If you have obtained performance rights to this title, please refer to your licensing agreement for important billing and credit requirements.

ALABASTER was first produced by Florida Repertory Theatre (Greg Longenhagen, Artistic Director; John Martin, Executive Director) in Fort Myers, Florida on December 20, 2019 as the first of an eleven-theatre National New Play Network Rolling World Premiere. The production was directed by Jason Parrish, with a scenic design by Richard Crowell, costume design by Charlene Gross, lighting and projection design by Rob Siler, sound design by Katie Lowe, and original outsider folk art by Sara Morsey. The production stage manager was Ruth E. Kramer. The cast was as follows:

JUNE . . . . Rachel Burttram
ALICE . . . . Dana Brooke
WEEZY . . . . Carolyn Messina
BIB . . . . Sara Morsey

ALABASTER then received an eleven-theater National New Play Network Rolling World Premiere with support from the David Goldman Fund for New American Plays. Participating Theaters: Capital Stage (Sacramento, California), 16th Street Theater (Berwyn, Illinois), Kitchen Dog Theater (Dallas, Texas), Shrewd Productions (Austin, Texas), Know Theatre of Cincinnati (Cincinnati, Ohio), Phoenix Theatre (Indianapolis, Indiana), Williamston Theatre (Williamston, Michigan), Salt Lake Acting Company (Salt Lake City, Utah), New Jersey Repertory Company (Long Branch, New Jersey), and Oregon Contemporary Theatre (Eugene, Oregon).

CHARACTERS

ALICE – a renowned photographer
JUNE – an Alabama outsider artist
WEEZY – a goat (and daughter to Bib)
BIB – a very old goat (and mother to Weezy)

Neither Bib nor Weezy should be dressed like goats. While they may have the occasional goat "feature," mostly they walk and talk just like humans. The goats are not caricatures. They are as real as any human. They have their own goat language, which – in moments of joy and grief and everything in between – is genuine and specific. They *bleat* and *bah* as goats do, with intention, creating a real dialogue between characters. We should be able to see their faces, their expressions, etc. This is vital.

SETTING

Somewhere near Alabaster, Alabama, mid-July. Portrait of an old farmhouse, mid-morning. The focal point is a master bedroom. An assemblage of outsider art, stacks of barn wood, and art supplies fill the corners of this sun-lit room along with a large old bed. The room should look more like a working art studio than an art gallery.

Also in this picture is a yard, a porch, and a space for Weezy and Bib (a pallet of straw and a small goat barn).

This place, a virtual canvas, gains color and crispness as the story moves along, reflecting at any moment the mood or perspective of what the players experience as well as their point of view through the "viewfinder." Projections are encouraged but not required.

TIME

Present day.

AUTHOR'S NOTES

This is not a *friendly* farm. Death is known to the inhabitants of this realm and to the creatures lured into its clutches in a way that changes them forever. In this story, which spans a single day, we are experiencing four "women," each at a crossroads, each facing a wall of fire. Though at times it may seem like they are simply exchanging pleasantries, they are quite literally <u>fighting for their lives</u>. In "come to Jesus" moments like these, worn down by the never-ending savage blows of life, we are faced with our own mortality. We understand time as a luxury. Weezy is an all-seeing, all-knowing instrument of *the Divine*. She is of another realm and of a higher purpose.

In this world. On this day. The time for pleasantries is <u>over</u>.

Resist the urge to play things "nice."

Important Note: The scars (predominantly seen on June's face and back) may be manifested in any number of ways (e.g. prosthetics, tattoos, or even projections); so long as they and the SEVERITY of them are CLEARLY visible to the audience. This is not negotiable. This is a play about scars. Do not attempt this play unless you can commit to the scars.

For Carolyn
my rock...
my barkeep...
my hero...

ACT I

Scene One

(AT RISE: Saturday, mid-morning. **WEEZY** *enters the light. She addresses the audience as she addresses nearly everyone else around her: with a neutral, no-nonsense, no-bullshit tone.)*

WEEZY. *(More dry than convivial.)* My name is Weezy, I am a goat, I am aware that I am a goat.

(Looking around at the audience.)

We are presently on a small farm in the backwoods of North *Alabama.*

(Beat.)

So *that's* happenin.

(Beat.)

We are in –

(The unmistakable sound of a goat is heard.)

BIB. *(From off.)* Mmaaahaaaahaaaaaahaaah!

WEEZY. We'll get through it together.

(Beat.)

We are in *Alabaster,* Alabama. Right near Gip's Place,* of which you might have heard, the last remainin juke joint in the state of Alabama. It's BYOB, which's nothin

---

* Mr. Gip passed away during the premiere of this play. The future of Gip's Place is unknown.

to do with this story, but is useful information on a Friday night.

> (**BIB**, *a very old goat, slightly disoriented (possible dementia), enters and calls to* **WEEZY**.)

BIB. Maahaaaahaahaa...

> (**BIB** *walks toward* **WEEZY**.)

Maaaaaah...

WEEZY. *(To the audience.)* That's my mama. *Bib.*

> (**BIB** *notices the audience. She is highly put out at the sight of so many unexpected visitors. She looks at* **WEEZY** *and back at the audience.)*

We don't get many visitors.

BIB. *(To* **WEEZY** – *"What's all this,* Field of Dreams*?")* Mmah-Maaah...

> (*During the following,* **BIB** *works her way across the yard to her pallet at the goat barn giving certain audience members a suspicious side-eye and griping along the way. At times, she stops and re-routes herself. It is obvious she has directional issues.* **WEEZY** *helps* **BIB** *along as necessary (ad lib) using directional comments (i.e., "Around the garden, Mama... right.")*

WEEZY. *(To the audience.)* She's sick. Old and sick.
(To **BIB**.*)* You stay off those beet greens, Mama, you know how they like to repeat on ya.
(To the audience.) I didn't always know my mama. I was taken from her when I was real little.

> (**BIB** *settles onto her pallet.)*

I have no memory of her from before. But she's here now. Right.
(To **BIB**.*)* OK, Mama?

*(**BIB** closes her eyes.)*

(Lights up on a large sunlit bedroom filled with stacks of barn wood, paintings, cans of house paint, and art supplies. On the bed, a woman sits dressed in a robe, nervously sipping from a coffee mug and looking anxiously around the room. Her face, arms, shoulders, torso, back, and legs are covered in scars (puncture wounds, abrasions, gashes, and surgical scars).)

(To the audience.) That's June. June and me, we have a connection.

*(To **JUNE**.)* Right, June?

*(**JUNE** shoots **WEEZY** "the bird" then goes back to looking around the room nervously. In the midst of all this, there are camera bags, video and lighting equipment lying around the room.)*

*(A photographer (**ALICE**) enters the bedroom as if returning from a related task. She begins setting up her tripod and video camera, pointing it in the direction of the bed.)*

And that's a new person. She's not from around here.

*(To **JUNE**.)* Just remember, June. You asked her to come.

*(**JUNE** nods nervously in response.)*

*(Note: **JUNE** and **WEEZY** are able to see and hear each other as if there were no walls between them. For the duration of the play, **WEEZY** moves wherever she likes; she has full command of the stage, and sits and walks wherever necessary to communicate with and observe the other players. Her default position, however, is in the lawn chair next to her ailing mother, **BIB**. **ALICE** is unaware of **WEEZY**'s presence.)*

(**WEEZY** *tucks* **BIB** *into bed and watches the action unfold, eating popcorn, drinking beer, and occasionally commenting on the scene to the players and sometimes directly to the audience, as if watching a daytime soap.*)

JUNE. *(Nervously.)* Did you get somethin to eat? People talk about eatin when they don't know what to talk about.

ALICE. I had a snack on the plane.

JUNE. Never been on a plane. I don't really know anybody I could fly to, anyway. Well, I know you now, I could fly to you. Times Square, maybe.

ALICE. See a show?

JUNE. Nah. I wanna eat *street food.* Mystery meat. On *sticks.* Stand there in the middle of it, feel big or feel small.

> *(Beat.)*

You live in Brooklyn right?

> (**JUNE** *takes a sip from her coffee mug.*)

ALICE. That's debatable.
> *(Off* **JUNE***'s look.)* I'm kind of sorting that out.

> *(Beat.)*

Is that coffee?

JUNE. Variation on coffee.

ALICE. What's the variation?

JUNE. I use Bourbon instead.

ALICE. Instead of / what?

JUNE. *(Overlapping.)* Instead of coffee.

> (**JUNE** *offers* **ALICE** *a sip.*)

ALICE. Tempting.

JUNE. Gotta be somewhere.

ALICE. It's the work, ya know?

JUNE. The *work.*

ALICE. Nothing personal.

JUNE. Do you know Annie Leibovitz?

ALICE. I do know Annie.

JUNE. What's she like?

ALICE. She's hilarious. And very real. And miles ahead.

JUNE. I read some place it's the photographer's job to make their subjects comfortable. She does not...*subscribe* to this notion.

ALICE. *(Playfully.)* Well, we're not *wedding planners.* I'm not supposed to console you, I'm supposed to *capture* you.

JUNE. *(Suggestively.)* I bet that was meant to sound dangerous.

ALICE. *(Playing along.)* Did it not sound dangerous?

JUNE. It did not sound dangerous.

ALICE. OK, define dangerous.

JUNE. *(Sipping from her mug.)* Clowns. Banana slugs. *Me.*

　　　　(Beat.)

We used to let outsiders just come and go but things have gotten so desperate.

ALICE. *(Playing along.)* Oh yeah?

JUNE. It's the inbreedin, we lay traps.

　　　(Suggestively.) Amazin what we catch.

ALICE. Really...?

JUNE. *Really.*

　　　　(Pause.)

ALICE. *(Suggestively.)* What do you use for bait?

　　　　(An electric pause.)

　　　　*(Interrupting cell phone: **ALICE**'s phone rings with some VERY UNPLEASANT RINGTONE.)*

JUNE. Who the fuck is on your shit list?

ALICE. My dad.

JUNE. *Solid.*

> (**ALICE** *digs for the phone in her backpack and dismisses the call.*)

ALICE. Sorry.

JUNE. Alice?

ALICE. Yeah?

JUNE. Breathe.

ALICE. That's my line.

> (**ALICE** *takes a deep cleansing breath.* **JUNE**, **WEEZY**, *and* **BIB** *(almost in unison) take a deep cleansing breath*.*)

JUNE. You need a break?

ALICE. I'm good.

> (**ALICE** *resumes setting up her equipment.*)

JUNE. So, how many women have you...ya know...

ALICE. You're number seven.

JUNE. Lucky seven. You just go from city to city...

ALICE. Pretty much.

JUNE. *(Intentionally ambiguous.)* Got a favorite?

ALICE. Savannah.

JUNE. *(Playfully.)* Is she pretty?

ALICE. What – oooh, you're asking me to pick a favorite *woman.*

JUNE.	**ALICE**.
Sure.	No way.

JUNE. *(A new tack.)* Do they all have scars like me?

> *(Pause.)*

Guess not.

ALICE. What are you asking?

JUNE. I thought that was pretty straight forward.

---

* *Breathing* is an important and recurring motif in this play. These moments lead us into new territory and create a togetherness, an *intimacy*. All breaths should be audible to the audience.

ALICE. Ya think?

JUNE. *(Dryly.)* I don't know what to think, I'm makin shit up.

ALICE. What was the question?

> *(**WEEZY** keeps her attention focused on the action but talks for the benefit of the audience. She may rise from her chair and enter the playing space or the audience space when it suits her.)*

WEEZY. *(To the audience.)* June likes to push.

JUNE. *(To **ALICE**.)* Do they all...have scars...like me?

WEEZY. *(To the audience.)* I used to think it was the PTSD from her injuries, but then I remembered, nope, she's always been a bitch.

> *(The energy of the conversation now takes on a more adversarial tone as **JUNE** begins to "push.")*

JUNE. *(To **ALICE**.)* Hello?

ALICE. No and yes.

JUNE. Good answer, / duh.

ALICE. *(Overlapping.)* It's not about the scars.

JUNE. You're takin pictures of people with scars but it's not about the scars, what's it about, then, Alice, tell me.

ALICE. *(Pointedly.)* I think it might be hard to tell *you* anything.

> *(Beat.)*

I dunno, *fear*?

JUNE. Rings a bell.

WEEZY. *(Directed mostly at **JUNE**.)* Fear of the unknown, fear of self-discovery, fear of *happiness*, even.

ALICE. These women – some of / these women are –

JUNE. *(Overlapping.)* Why not men?

ALICE. *(Overlapping – continuous.)* ...in a lot of pain because – NO. *Men?* Why do people / always ask me that?

JUNE. *(Overlapping.)*	WEEZY. *(Overlapping.)*
It's whatever, do / your thing.	*(To* JUNE.*)* Let her talk!

ALICE. *(Overlapping.)* Can I finish?

      (Pause.)

It's not about the scars, / the scars are a way in.

JUNE. *(Overlapping.)* You're gonna tell me / they're beautiful?

WEEZY. *(Overlapping – exasperated, under her breath.)* Oh my God.

      (ALICE *waits for* JUNE *to settle.)*

ALICE. They're a way *in*.

JUNE. *In.*

ALICE. I want to be careful here because it's not like I'm an expert on scars or anything, but – what I'm learning is...every scar, every woman, is *different*. Some women are still in the early stages, others have...made peace? I guess? *(Softening.)* With their physical worlds?

JUNE. And now you're in it.

ALICE. I feel pretty lucky. Not everyone gets to do what I do.

JUNE. *(Calculating.)* Why the switch?

ALICE. *Switch?*

JUNE. From the celebrities.

ALICE. My assignment work, you mean?

JUNE. *(Put off by the choice of words.)* Assignment. Work.

JUNE.	ALICE.
I'm not painting you in.*	Have you been reading my diary?

ALICE. I needed a change.

JUNE. Just all of a sudden...

      (Beat.)

---

* I'm not trying to paint you into a corner with your art; it's your art, your prerogative.

You spend just as much time with Demi Moore as someone like me, what's the difference, really?

ALICE. Is that a serious question? It's more intimate, obviously.

JUNE. Not obviously. I've seen your celebrity shots, those are some scarred up motherfuckers.

ALICE. I can see I have to choose my words more carefully.

JUNE. Because you weren't before?

ALICE. That's not how I meant it.

JUNE. It's how *I* meant it.

ALICE. I'm listening.

JUNE. Why...the switch?

ALICE. I told you, I needed a change.

JUNE.	**ALICE.**
You needed a change because you needed a change?	And it was admittedly a pat response, but it's what people say in polite company instead of the alternative.
I'm not polite company.	Which is the horrible truth of their *lives*.

(Beat.)

ALICE. Is that OK? Is that OK, June? If I hang back on that question. Until I know you? A little better?

(Beat.)

JUNE. *(Bratty.)* I think you would make a <u>*shitty*</u> weddin planner.

WEEZY. *(Disapprovingly – throwing popcorn at* **JUNE**.*)* Booooh!!!! Boooooooooh!!!

JUNE. *(To* **WEEZY**.*)* Would you – I got it!

ALICE. Got what?

JUNE. *(To* **ALICE**, *self-correcting.)* I've got...an *apology*.

WEEZY. *(To* **JUNE**.*)* Asshole.

ALICE. No. Actually, I'm sorry. Can we start over?

JUNE. Sure.

ALICE. Great.

> (**WEEZY** *enters the bedroom area and uncovers a pile of paintings as* **ALICE** *looks up and around at the art in the room.*)

I love all your pieces.

JUNE. Thanks.

ALICE. I haven't had a good look, but I'd like to.

JUNE. Sure.

ALICE. *(Positioning the camera.)* Did I see Jim Sudduth over there? You're a collector, obviously. I collect a bit myself.

JUNE. Am I *scar-ier* than Hollywood?

> (**ALICE** *adjusts the light on* **JUNE**. **JUNE** *watches her.*)

ALICE. By an order of magnitude. But, I wouldn't come all this way just to cower in a corner.

JUNE. You can if you want to.

ALICE. I don't want to.

JUNE. You don't want to?

ALICE. *(Pointedly.)* I don't want to.

> *(Another electric pause.)*

You answered my ad.

JUNE. Oh, that was my neighbor, Peachy Sawgrass.

ALICE.	**JUNE**.
Peachy Sawgrass.	She told me – I know, it's a name – she told me you were lookin for women.

ALICE. Ah. I guess you found it online?

JUNE. I don't do *online*. I'm dumb and I have a dumb phone and I like it that way.

ALICE. *(Stunned.) Really?*

JUNE. No shit.

ALICE. So…if you don't do *online,* how did you find *me*?

JUNE. *("Duh.")* The library.

ALICE. Your local library has my books?

JUNE. Birmingham. I called Aggie Nolan at the Five Points branch, she sends me stuff.

ALICE. You have your own personal librarian?

JUNE. She's my cousin, she's also a librarian, she told me she saw your pictures one time at the Corcoran when she went up there on a school trip to DC. She wanted me to ask you why people in your pictures look so sad all the time and then I looked at your pictures and I saw it too. The sadness, I mean. Or maybe that's new information. To you?

(Beat.)

Are you gay?

WEEZY. *(To **JUNE**.)* OH MY GOD.

ALICE. You ask a lot of questions.

WEEZY. *(To **JUNE**.)* SERIOUSLY?

JUNE. Are you?

ALICE. Does it matter?

JUNE. No.

(Beat.)

Are you attracted to me?

(Pause.)

ALICE. No. No, I'm not attracted to you.

JUNE. Really?

ALICE. You're not my type.

JUNE.	**WEEZY**.
DAMN! Not. Your. Type?!	NICE!
Wow...	*(To **JUNE**.)* You deserved that one.
*(Mostly to **WEEZY**.)* Whatever.	She's just tryin to do her *job,* June. Would you relax?

JUNE. *(Bratty. Half to* **WEEZY**, *half to* **ALICE**.) *Assignments and clients and jobs. Oh, my.*

ALICE. You're pretty impossible.

JUNE. So many words.

ALICE. Maybe we should stay focused on the work.

JUNE. Yeah, OK.

ALICE. Are you ready?

JUNE. Born ready.

> (**ALICE** *sits in a chair next to the video camera and pulls out a note pad and a pen. Despite all of* **JUNE***'s bravado, she now becomes visibly nervous, as one would at a dentist's office when implements of torture become visible to the patient.)*

ALICE. OK. So, these questions...just say skip, OK, if you can't or don't want to answer.

JUNE. Skip?

ALICE. Yeah. Ya know, like if I ask you –

JUNE. NEXT QUESTION!

> *(Beat.)*

My head pops off from time to time, just to warn ya.

> (**JUNE** *turns to see* **WEEZY** *amused but shaking her head with disappointment. She sticks her tongue out at* **WEEZY**.)

> (**ALICE** *smiles at* **JUNE** *who takes a big breath.* **ALICE** *follows with a big breath.* **WEEZY**, *not wanting to be rude, takes a reluctant breath.* **BIB**, *still snoozing, takes a sleepy staccato-style catch-up breath and then exhales softly.)*

ALICE. You're very brave, sitting there. OK...just so you know the order, I'm going to ask about the scars first so I can get the video. We'll do the photographs separately when we get the light.

JUNE. Fine.

>*(**ALICE** turns on the video camera. **JUNE** nervously mugs for the camera.)*

I don't know why I did that, there's nobody in there.

>*(**ALICE** turns on her little handheld voice recorder. She looks up to see that **JUNE** has lowered her robe. **JUNE**'s arms, shoulders, chest, and torso are visible now, and covered with scars.)*

>*(Beat.)*

ALICE. Oh. No. I'm only recording from the / shoulders up. You can...

>*(Beat.)*

JUNE. Why am I so quick to take my clothes off, Alice? That is somethin I should explore.

>*(Pause.)*

ALICE. Are you more comfortable with your clothes off?

JUNE.	**WEEZY**.
That is...	YES.
Yes. Yes, I am.	

ALICE. Well, it certainly doesn't bother me, whatever makes you happy.

>*(**JUNE** opens her mouth to make a comment.)*

WEEZY. *(Not amused.)* GIRL, GET DRESSED!

>*(**JUNE** rolls her eyes at **WEEZY** and then, just to fuck with her, she <u>slowly</u> pulls her robe back up over her shoulders and ties it closed.)*

ALICE. This is June.

JUNE. *(Tentatively. Leaning into the microphone.)* Hello.

ALICE. It's July 12, 2019, and we're just outside Alabaster, Alabama.

JUNE. Lord, that's almost my gravestone.

ALICE. So, how long have you lived here, June?

JUNE. All my life. Which is forever, seems like forever.

ALICE. You like living here?

JUNE. I like the farm.

ALICE. The farm.

JUNE. I don't get out much.

ALICE. Why's that?

JUNE.	**WEEZY.**
Issues.	*Issues.*

ALICE. Issues. Anything / interesting?

JUNE. *(Overlapping.)* Next.

ALICE. Got it. So, what do you do for a living?

JUNE. That's a stupid question.

ALICE. I'm sorry?

JUNE. No, I get it. I get it. It's a progression.

>   *(Beat.)*

> I take care of the farm. Feed the goats. Whatever needs
> doin. I don't really need a whole lot...

ALICE. Are you –

JUNE. *(Continuous.)* actually...

> *(A sort of fog washes over **JUNE**. She looks to*
> ***WEEZY** for support. **WEEZY** returns a steady*
> *gaze. In moments like these, **WEEZY** acts as a*
> *sort of emotional support animal for **JUNE**;*
> *she often "clocks" **JUNE**'s PTSD triggers long*
> *before **JUNE** does.)*

ALICE. *(Tentatively.)* So...you're happy?

>   *(Beat.)*

> Last week, when we spoke on the phone, you were
> telling me about the accident.

JUNE. *(To **ALICE** – still looking at **WEEZY**.) Accident?*

WEEZY. *(To **JUNE** – "Relax, it's just a word.")* Accident.

JUNE. *(To **ALICE** – still looking at **WEEZY**.)* When you say
accident, I think maybe we're talkin about a fender
bender on the bypass.

ALICE. I'm so sorry. I was just trying to be sensitive.

JUNE. *(To **ALICE** – still looking at **WEEZY**.)* Could you not, you're creepin me out.

> *(**JUNE** now turns her focus back to **ALICE**.)*

(Softening.) Sorry. We don't have to dance around it.

ALICE. OK.

> *(Beat.)*

There was a storm?

> *(The video camera beeps. **JUNE** startles.)*

JUNE. *(Very unsettled now.)* You could say that.

> *(The beeping continues. **ALICE** becomes momentarily distracted trying to silence the noise.)*

WEEZY. *(To **JUNE**.)* Breathe.

> *(The beeping continues. **JUNE** hears more than the beeping. In her head she can see the color red flashing on and off and hear the sound of something like a loud FACTORY ALARM. The audience sees and hears whatever **JUNE** does. **ALICE** hears only the beeping of the camera.)*

ALICE. *(Oblivious to **JUNE**'s agitated state.)* And you were here, right? On the farm?

> *(The beeping continues. **JUNE**'s heart is pounding. **ALICE** struggles with the camera.)*

Shit. It's not stopping!

> *(The beeping stops. The alarm in **JUNE**'s head is replaced with the sound of a LOW MENACING HUM or GLASS SLOWLY SCRAPING AGAINST HARD WOOD FLOOR.)*

Oh, there we go. God. I hate that thing.

> *(**ALICE** collects herself and turns her focus back to **JUNE**.)*

So sorry. OK. Umm...*right*. You lost your family? They were...*crushed*?

> (**JUNE** *is now experiencing a full-blown PTSD episode. We now hear the sound of a low menacing hum or glass slowly scraping against a hard wood floor. This continues during the following.*)

JUNE. (*Cold as ice. She speaks calmly, but her rage and anger fuel the onslaught.*) You need to trust me, don't you?

WEEZY. (*To* **JUNE**, *preemptively.*) OK.

ALICE. (*To* **JUNE**.) What?

JUNE. You need to trust me...

WEEZY. (*Overlapping.*) She's just tryin to do her job, June.

JUNE. (*Continuous.*) ...because you want your story to be accurate because it's just too hard to believe / or whatever

WEEZY. (*Overlapping.*) Why do you have to be such a ball-buster / all the time,

JUNE. (*Overlapping – continuous.*) but I could be unstable, right, I could just be some redneck meth head, / for all you know,

WEEZY. (*Overlapping – continuous.*) just let her do her / job.

JUNE. (*Overlapping – continuous.*) lookin for my payday, my fifteen minutes, and embarrass the / hell outta you

WEEZY. (*Overlapping.*) Let. Her do. / Her job!

JUNE. (*Overlapping – continuous.*) like that *lyin shitball* did to Oprah Winfrey.

ALICE. *A Million Little* / *Pieces...*

JUNE. (*Overlapping.*) A million little SHITBALL pieces.

ALICE. June. I came a long way to be here today and I'm sitting here with you now and there are scars all over your body, every *part*...of your body. I just want to know what happened.

JUNE. For your coffee table book, fancy New York friends.

ALICE. You know, June, I have scars too.

JUNE. That's hot. Are we in a club now?

ALICE. I'm on your side.

JUNE. *(Nauseated by the syllables.) On – your – side?* Who the fuck are you, Jerry Lewis?

      (Begin rapid fire.)

WEEZY. She could go,

JUNE. Are you Alice, are you?

WEEZY. you could just ask her to go.

JUNE. If you were passin through this shit town on your way to sunny Orlando and you saw me sittin on a bench outside of Golden Corral, and you wanted to take my picture.

WEEZY. Or just let her sit here.

JUNE.	**WEEZY**.
Would you ask my name and buy me a coffee,	In your creepy bedroom.
or is that just too much	And get eaten alive, Slowly and painfully.
of a CHORE?	BY A WEIRDO!

JUNE. On *your side*. You know somethin, I was valedictorian of my high school class, you believe that? That's all right though, just sit there...with your / assumptions.

WEEZY. *(Overlapping – to **JUNE** – exasperated now.)* OK. OK!

JUNE. *(To **WEEZY**.)* No. No. NOT OK.

ALICE. "*My*" assumptions?

JUNE. *(To **ALICE**.)* Maybe you should go. If you know where you're goin. Do you know?

ALICE. *(Overlapping.)* So lost. / Sooo lost.

JUNE. Where you're / goin? To?

WEEZY. *(Overlapping – to **JUNE**.)* June. JUNE! <u>KNOCK IT OFF</u>!!!!!

(End rapid fire.)

*(**JUNE** startles, as if waking up from a nightmare. The red lights and the noises in her head finally quiet. She glares at **WEEZY**. She looks at **ALICE**, horrified and confused at her own behavior.)*

JUNE. I – I am so sorry. Did I – can we – can we just... umm...slow down for a minute?

ALICE. Absolutely. Yes. Yes.

JUNE. OK...

*(**ALICE**'s phone rings again with the same VERY UNPLEASANT RINGTONE.)*

ALICE. Fuck! Fucking phone.

JUNE. *(Dryly.)* What if like you changed it to somethin from *Sound of Music*, could that be a thing?

ALICE. I'm sorry.

*(**ALICE** swipes at the phone and dismisses the call.)*

JUNE. *(A realization.)* Oh my God.

*(Half to **ALICE**, half to **WEEZY**.)*

This is just like *Bridges of Madison County*.

WEEZY. *(Dryly – to **JUNE**.)* It's not like *Bridges of Madison County*.

(Begin rapid fire.)

JUNE. *(To **WEEZY**.)* It is.

WEEZY. *(To **JUNE**.)* No it's not.

JUNE. *(To **WEEZY**.)* Yes it is.

WEEZY. *(To **JUNE**.)* No it's not.

JUNE. *(To **WEEZY**.)* Yes it fuckin is!

*(To **ALICE**.)* You're Clint Eastwood.

WEEZY. *(Hissing.)* NO! She's *not*!

JUNE. *(To **ALICE**.)* Are we gonna sleep together?

(End rapid fire. Beat.)

ALICE. *(Coldly.)* It's not a coffee table book. Also, you don't know my life.

> *(Pause.* **JUNE** *makes an attempt at an apology but is still very confused about how she slipped into such a rage.)*

JUNE. I'm sorry / I don't know what...

WEEZY. *(Overlapping – to* **JUNE**.*)* The camera was beepin.

> *(***JUNE** *turns to look at* **WEEZY**.*)*

(Repeating.) The *camera*...was <u>*beepin*</u>.

JUNE. What – oh! Yeah! It was *beepin*!

(To **ALICE**.*)* The camera was beepin.

(Reacting to **ALICE***'s puzzled look.)* The camera was beepin and I...

> *(***JUNE** *taps a bit on her head to indicate her PTSD.)*

ALICE. *(Slowly – a realization.)* Oh! Oh...and I – oh, I'm sorry. I'm so sorry, it was beeping and I got distracted. *Shit.* I'm sorry, June.

JUNE. No, ya know what, you're here, and you're great, and I have a lot of...

WEEZY. Blockers.

JUNE. *Blockers ("issues")*. So. You're great...you're –

> *(***JUNE** *looks at* **ALICE** *with the ache of a thousand years. Pause.)*

ALICE. *(Tenderly.)* June...

JUNE. Alice...

ALICE. *(Tenderly.)* It's OK, you know?

JUNE. What?

ALICE. To...be *direct* and *ask*...for the things you want.

JUNE. Right. What do I want?

ALICE. *Intimacy?* Guessing.

JUNE. *Intimacy*...

> *(***JUNE** *thinks about the word for a moment. She works through the puzzle...)*

(Processing out loud.)

Right, right. I answered your ad... Oh, wow. I [think I] know why I did that. It's what you're sayin but I didn't see it and now I see it.

*(Looking up at **ALICE**.)*

I *wanted* you here.

ALICE. Me, specifically?

JUNE. It was somethin about your pictures. The *sadness.* You know that thing when you feel somebody so close and you don't even know 'em, but it's there, that feelin – that's probably what they call stalkin – but ya know what I mean? And you made it easy, you came to me, I didn't even have to stand outside your house or even dig in your dumpster.

> *(**JUNE** looks at **ALICE** intently. **ALICE** does not flinch.)*

How on Earth are you gonna deal with me?

ALICE. *Riot gear* comes to mind.

JUNE. But I'm cute, right?

> *(An electric pause. **JUNE** keeps her eyes locked on **ALICE** as she comments on the camera.)*

That camera is just rollin and rollin huh?

> *(**ALICE**, with her eyes fixed on **JUNE**, turns off the video camera.)*

ALICE. I wasn't trying to avoid you before.

JUNE. Before?

ALICE. Yeah, you asked me a question, / and I didn't –

JUNE. *(Overlapping – remembering.)* Oh, yeah. Keepin a safe distance.

ALICE. That sounds horrible. It's, umm...it's just really REALLY important that I don't get too close.

JUNE. What happens if you get too close, Alice? *(Suggestively.)* Is that a thing?

ALICE. I wasn't specifically talking about sex.

JUNE. *(Amused.)* Oh, you thought I was talkin about sex?

ALICE. Weren't you?

WEEZY. YES.

> *(Beat.)*

ALICE. No, I've never done that.

JUNE. What, you mean crossed a line with a client? Well that makes two of us.

> *(Pointedly.)* We can just *not-do-that* together.

ALICE. *(Amused.)* You *do* like to push.

> *(**WEEZY** stares at **JUNE**, "told ya so.")*

JUNE. *(To **WEEZY**.)* Shut up. *(To **ALICE**.)* Are you gonna take my picture?

> *(**ALICE** looks around and determines the natural light in the room is just perfect for photographs.)*

ALICE. Actually. Yeah, let's do that.

> *(During the following, **ALICE** rearranges equipment and small furnishings. She takes a few test shots, using her light meter to adjust the exposure on her camera. Again, **JUNE** becomes somewhat nervous at the sight of the camera equipment. She suggests a word game – a sort of "Twenty Questions" – to take her mind off of it.)*

JUNE. *(Nervously.)* Tell me things.

ALICE. *Things.*

JUNE. Yeah, but not like stupid things, let's…let's, umm, let's do that thing, like a game, OK, like I'll say somethin and then you say somethin.

ALICE. *(Making an allusion to their "how do you define dangerous" conversation from before.) This* sounds dangerous.

JUNE. It is, yes, and no follow-ups.

ALICE. No follow-ups.

JUNE. Right. Like, OK... I'll just go. Umm...*butter pecan.* That is technically a stupid thing, but it's ice cream and therefore, it is deadly serious.

ALICE. I – mint chocolate chip?

JUNE. Big guns! OK. OK. *(Thinking of a hard question.)* Mary Ann or Ginger?

ALICE. *(Unflinching.)* Mary Ann, all day.

      (Beat.)

JUNE. I really thought that would be a hard question.

ALICE. It's not a hard question.

      (Long pause. Begin rapid fire.)

JUNE. *(Off* **ALICE***'s look.)* Oh! It's me now?

ALICE. Your rule.

JUNE. What?

ALICE. *Mary Ann or Ginger?*

JUNE. Never thought / about it.

WEEZY. *(To* **JUNE***.)* Ginger.

ALICE. *(To* **JUNE***.)* You lie!

JUNE. *(To* **ALICE***.)* Well, I've – I mean Tom Selleck or Brad Pitt, ya know, but this is way different.

ALICE. But it's not.

JUNE. It is.

WEEZY. *(To* **JUNE***.)* Ginger.

ALICE. *(To* **JUNE***.)* It's not.

JUNE. It is.

ALICE. Who would you rather?

JUNE. No follow-ups!

WEEZY. *(To* **JUNE***.)* Just answer the question!

ALICE. *(To* **JUNE***.)* There's nothin to follow, you haven't even answered the question.

JUNE. Fuck it, I don't / know.

WEEZY. *(Overlapping, calling to* **JUNE** *– as if watching an easy sports play about to go horribly wrong.)* GINGER, OH MY GOD, <u>GINGER</u>!

JUNE. I've never been with a girl, how would I –

ALICE. *(Overlapping – flatly.)* You're picturing it right / now, aren't you?

WEEZY. *(Overlapping.)* GINGERRRRRRRR!

JUNE. *(Overlapping.)* Ginger. Fuckin Ginger. She's tall, she could like *do* things.

ALICE. Fuck yeah.

JUNE. *(To both **ALICE** and **WEEZY**.)* Happy now?

> *(End rapid fire. **ALICE** walks over to **JUNE** and asks permission to drape her robe a certain way, exposing her arms and shoulders. She adjusts **JUNE***'s position on the bed.)*

ALICE. Can you push back a little. There. OK. Drop your shoulders. Great.

> *(**ALICE** takes a picture. Note to sound designer: We may hear a sound every time she takes a picture, but it needn't be a "camera click" sound per se.)*

JUNE. New topic. OK. So, *Survivor* calls and you're dropped / on a deserted island.

ALICE. *(Overlapping.)* Survivor?

> *(Positioning **JUNE**.)*

Chin down.

> *(Another picture.)*

JUNE. The TV show *Survivor* calls and you're dropped on a deserted island.

ALICE. OK.

JUNE. What is your *one luxury item*?

ALICE. Food truck.

JUNE. *(Suddenly highly aroused.)* Shit. Food truck's not fuckin around.

ALICE. Nope.

JUNE. *(Mesmerized by the idea.)* What kinda food truck?

ALICE. Korean BBQ.

JUNE. Why?

ALICE. Because I love Korean food and I love BBQ.

JUNE. OutSTANDING.

ALICE. Chin down again. Great.

> *(A picture.)*

JUNE. Hmm.

ALICE. What about you?

JUNE. Probably a sleepin bag. Wait, I'm on TV? OK, eyeliner. Chapstick.

ALICE. Just one.

JUNE. What – you brought a whole *food truck*!

ALICE. Still just one thing.

JUNE. I don't think that's true.

> *(A picture. **ALICE** positions **JUNE** again. Exposing her legs this time.)*

ALICE. Just turn slightly. Yeah. Head back. Can you wrap your arms – great, great.

> *(A picture.)*

You're allowed one thing.

JUNE. Fine. A makeup bag. Filled with eyeliner, chapstick. Whatever else I can fit in there, tacos, maybe, or taco salad, and one of those *spoon-fork* things.

WEEZY. Spork.

ALICE. Spork?

JUNE. *Spork,* hot sauce.

ALICE. There's no way you're gonna get away with that.

JUNE. *We'll see.*

> *(A picture. **JUNE** thinks of another question while absently humming a tune…)*

ALICE. Least favorite subject?

JUNE. Chemistry.

ALICE. PE.

JUNE. *(Words tumbling.)* Can I change my answer, PE, then chemistry, daddy was a deacon.

ALICE. Photographer.

JUNE. Mama was crazy.

> *(A picture. Begin rapid fire.)*

ALICE. Mine's dead.

JUNE. Switch.

ALICE. I'm an only child.

JUNE. Ditto.

ALICE. I want a house full of kids.

JUNE. Ditto!

ALICE. Three boys, three girls.

JUNE. *Brady Bunch*! Fuck, that's like a warehouse, sorry, no follow-ups.

> *(Beat.)*

SIX KIDS?!

> *(End rapid fire. Beat.)*

ALICE. My life is a tragedy.

> *(Beat.)*

JUNE. *(Softly.)* Ditto...

> *(A picture. **ALICE** turns **JUNE** around on the bed to face the wall. She lowers **JUNE**'s robe down to her waist, exposing the signs of <u>severe</u> trauma: her entire back is a tangled mass of gashes, abrusions, puncture wounds, and surgical scars.)*

> *(Silence.)*

ALICE. *(Visibly shaken.)* Shoulders...back.

JUNE. *(Brightly.)* Everything OK back there?

ALICE. It's going well, we're almost done.

JUNE. Good. You have a girl? Waitin at home.

ALICE. No.

JUNE. No?

ALICE. Not anymore.

JUNE. Where is she?

ALICE. She died.

> *(Positioning **JUNE**.)*

Chin up. A little more. Good.

> *(A picture.)*

JUNE. How?

ALICE. Car accident.

> *(A picture.)*

JUNE. When?

ALICE. Eleven months ago.

JUNE. Wait, what?

> *(A picture.)*

ALICE. She rented a car to drive to Vermont for a wedding.

JUNE. Whose weddin?

ALICE. Her mother's.

> *(A picture.)*

JUNE. Her mother's weddin?

> *(Beat.)*

She never made it?

ALICE. Somewhere in the mountains. There was a truck.

JUNE. A truck.

ALICE. Well...it's sketchy.

JUNE. No witnesses...

ALICE. Right, no witnesses. She, uh...she was four months pregnant. With our baby.

> *(Positioning **JUNE**.)*

Chin left. And your left shoulder up just – yes. Love that.

(A picture.)

JUNE. *(Tenderly.)* I'm so sorry, Alice.

ALICE. *(Lost in her own pain now.)* OK. I think we're done.

> (**JUNE** *pulls her robe back up over her shoulders. She turns to look at* **ALICE** *who is now scrolling through the pictures in the viewfinder of her camera.)*

JUNE. I ask a lotta questions. You OK?

> (**ALICE** *nods.*)

You're not OK. You don't have to – I'm sorry, I shoulda –

ALICE. *(Overlapping.)* It hurts. Some days…

> *(Beat.)*

She didn't die right away. So that's obviously kind of fucked up. To think about.

JUNE. Come here.

ALICE. I'm better now.

JUNE. How do you figure?

ALICE. Well, I'm here now. So.

> (**ALICE** *begins putting away her equipment.*)

JUNE. OK. Where were you yesterday?

> *(Begin rapid fire.)*

ALICE. In Savannah taking a picture.

JUNE. And before that?

ALICE. Charlotte. Roanoke. Virginia Beach.

JUNE. And before that?

ALICE. Allentown. Pittsburgh. These are really personal questions.

JUNE. *(Overlapping.)* And before that?

ALICE. Living with a friend.

JUNE. And before that?

ALICE. *(Words tumbling.)* Let me think – what was it – oh yeah – spa vacation out in Montauk.

(Beat.)

JUNE. *Rehab*. Nice.

(Beat.)

And before that?

ALICE. Stuffing my shit into storage. Out-of-control couch surfing.

JUNE. And before that?

ALICE. Just regular couch surfing.

JUNE.	**ALICE**.
And before that?	You ask the best questions. On assignment.

JUNE. Where?

ALICE. Madison Square Garden.

JUNE. Takin a picture?

ALICE. Evidently.

JUNE. Who was it?

ALICE. Doesn't matter.

JUNE. Madonna?

ALICE. Can't say.

JUNE. Lady Gaga. Justin Beiber.

(Beat.)

JUSTIN BEIBER???

*(**BIB** rouses out of a dead sleep at the prospect of seeing Justin Bieber. **WEEZY** uncovers a painting of a cat.)*

*(**ALICE** now notices the cat painting.)*

ALICE. *(Distractedly.)* I blacked out half way through.

*(**ALICE** picks up the cat painting, struck by its profound singularity.)*

JUNE. Shit.

ALICE. *(Half-distracted with the painting.)* And before that?

(Beat.)

Burying my daughter in Burlington...

JUNE. God...

> *(**ALICE** looks around at the other art in the room as if deciphering a puzzle.)*

ALICE. Where did you get all this?

JUNE. Alice?

ALICE. There's so much of it.

JUNE. *Around.* Alice?

ALICE. It's crazy good.

> *(Beat.)*

There's something...

> *(**ALICE** notices another painting in the corner of the room. She moves a few boxes to get a better look.)*

Wait, this doesn't –

JUNE. Doesn't what?

> *(**ALICE** looks at **JUNE**. Beat.)*

ALICE. Show me your hands.

> *(Beat.)*

Would you hold them up?

> *(**JUNE** holds up her hands. They are covered in dye and paint.)*

Oh, my God. How did I not –

> *(Beat.)*

This is *you*?

JUNE. Sure.

ALICE. Are you –

> *(**ALICE** picks up the painting.)*

But this isn't, I mean, this is – this is Jimmy Lee Sudduth...

JUNE. Who?

ALICE. *(Looking for a signature.)* He's an Alabama...

> *(During the following,* **JUNE** *changes out of her robe and into regular clothes.)*

> *(Dumbfounded.)*

You painted this?

JUNE. Did I say that?

> *(Beat.)*

What are you askin me, what the fuck?

> *(Beat.)*

What?!

ALICE. *(Referencing all of the art in the room.)* This is all you?

JUNE. Well, who else would it be, will you sit down, you're makin me nervous.

ALICE. No, I'm not going to be sitting down, June, you need representation. Have you really never been contacted by a curator or a collector?

JUNE. I sold a paintin to The Big Crab Shack in Birmingham once.

ALICE. Is that a gallery?

JUNE. It's a *CRAB SHACK, there's no mystery,* it's a crab shack!

WEEZY. *(To* **JUNE** *– a warning.)* OK.

JUNE. *(Annoyed.)* OK, Weezy! OK.

ALICE. Who's Weezy?

JUNE. I talk to goats.

ALICE. *(Playing along.)* Who doesn't?

> *("What the fuck?")*

What?

JUNE. It's a thing I do.

ALICE. Talk to goats?

> *(Beat.)*

And they talk back?

JUNE. Just Weezy.

ALICE. Just Weezy…

JUNE. Oh, I'm crazy.

WEEZY. *(To* **JUNE**.*)* She needed *that* out loud.

JUNE. *(To* **WEEZY**.*)* Outhouse rat, right Weezy?

ALICE. OK, who's Weezy?

WEEZY. *(To* **ALICE**.*)* I'm a goat.

JUNE. Did you hear that?

ALICE. Hear what?

JUNE. She's a goat.

ALICE. OK.

JUNE. *(A warning.)* You start hearin goats…

>*(Off* **ALICE***'s look.)*

Let's just hope you don't.

ALICE. Are they like…friendly goats?

JUNE. Nope.

>*(Beat.)*

>*(Begin rapid fire.)*

WEEZY. *(To* **JUNE**.*)* I'm friendly!

JUNE. *(To* **WEEZY**.*)* No you're not!

WEEZY. I'm friendly!

JUNE. You are deluded!

WEEZY. What the / fuck?

JUNE. *(Overlapping – continuous.)* Which is not anywhere / near the same thing as friendly. Not. Friendly.

WEEZY. *(Overlapping.)* I'm FUCKING FRIENDLY! I'm friendly as a motherfucker.

>*(End rapid fire.)*

JUNE. *(To* **ALICE**.*)* She's a friendly goat, just ask her.

ALICE. Where is she?

JUNE. Outside. Eatin up all my okra.

WEEZY. *(To* **JUNE**.*)* I'm not eatin your / okra!

JUNE. *(Overlapping. To* **WEEZY**.*)* You think I don't know who's eatin my okra?

WEEZY. It's the deer!

JUNE. *(To* **WEEZY**.*)* It's not the deer.

JUNE.	**WEEZY**.
(To **ALICE**.*)* It's not the deer.	*(To* **JUNE**.*)* It's the fuckin deer.

WEEZY. *(To* **JUNE**.*)* It fuckin is.

JUNE. *(Mouthing the words to* **ALICE**.*)* It's not.

> *(Beat.)*

Why are you still standin there holdin my picture?

ALICE. You need an agent. If you want your work out there, that's kind of how it is.

JUNE. *(Words tumbling.)* How it is – I've never accepted a human construct as *how it is* – it's not like *gravity* – gravity is how it is.

ALICE. You're right, you're right. That's absolutely one way to go with it, we can get you a tour.

> (**ALICE** *picks up another painting.)*

Jesus...the color.

JUNE. *(Increasingly irritated.)* Could you put that down please.

ALICE. *(Earnestly.)* Oh, I'm so sorry. Of course.

JUNE. I don't give a fuck, wear it on your head, you're not listenin. It's *not* for sale.

JUNE. *(Continuous.)*	**ALICE**.
I'm not for sale.	The –
I don't need anybody to come in here and tell me it's art, I know it's art.	How do you –

ALICE. It *is*.

JUNE. Thank you, I know that.

> (**WEEZY**, *now fed up with* **JUNE**'s *bullshit, is heard speaking in "goat" and making a loud racket outside* **JUNE**'s *window.)*

WEEZY. Maaaaah!!! Maaaaah!!!

ALICE. *(Bewildered.)* Goats?

> *(**WEEZY** peeks her head inside the window.
> **JUNE** is not amused.)*

JUNE. *(To **WEEZY**.)* Really, Weezy? Really?

WEEZY. *(Overlapping.)* Maaaaah!!!

JUNE. *(Overlapping.)* Exhibit A. This isn't friendly, this
is hostile and it's rude and you knew we were talkin,
which makes you an *ASS;* where's Bib?

WEEZY. MAAAAAAAAH!

> *(**ALICE** stands there stunned at the
> proceedings.)*

ALICE. What is she saying?

JUNE. *(Retrieving kibble from a nearby treat bucket.)* She's
talkin in goat, I have no fuckin idea.

WEEZY. *(Overlapping.)*   **ALICE**.
MAAAAAAAAH!   Am I on Mars?

JUNE. *(Overlapping.)* Time to feed the goats.

> *(**JUNE** hands a handful of kibble to **ALICE** to
> disperse. **ALICE** steps tentatively toward the
> window. **WEEZY** bumps at window frame
> from the outside.)*

WEEZY. MAAAAAAAAH!

ALICE. Jesus!

WEEZY. *(Innocently.)* Maaaah… Maaaah.

ALICE. Aww…look at her eyes. She's cute.

JUNE. *(To **ALICE**.)* She's fat.

WEEZY. *(To **JUNE**.)* YOU'RE FAT!
*(Innocently – to **ALICE**.)* Maaaah… Maaaah

ALICE. *(A greeting.)* Weezy…

> *(Beat.)*

Hello, Weezy.

> *(**ALICE** holds out a handful of kibble.)*

JUNE. Don't be scared. Don't be scared, just throw it at her, just – NOT LIKE THAT, SHE'LL RIP / YOUR FUCKIN ARM OFF!

WEEZY. *(Overlapping – to* **ALICE**, *half roar, half "bah.")* *RAAAAAAH!!!!!!!!!!*

> *(***ALICE*** *jumps backward, dropping the kibble out the window.)*

ALICE. Fuuuuuuuck!!!

> *(***JUNE*** *and* ***WEEZY*** *have a good laugh and high-five.)*

JUNE.	**WEEZY**.
Got us another one, Weezy!!!	BaaaaaaaaaaaHaHaHa HaHaHaHa!

> *(***BIB*** *has slowly made her way over to the window now. Meanwhile,* ***WEEZY*** *has gathered up all the treats and is eating them one by one, with no intention of sharing.)*

BIB. Maaah. Maaah.

JUNE. *(Sweetly.)* There's Miss Bib. Hey, Mama.

> *(Regarding the kibble.)*

Your treat's over there, go get it. Go, get it, woman.

(To **ALICE**.*)* Aww, this might be one of her bad days.

(Tenderly, to **BIB**.*)* Get your treat, you remember treats? Weezy's got your treat, Bib, you gon take that shit from her?

BIB. Maaah.

JUNE. Oh, Mama. Come here. Here, just take this one.

BIB. Maaah.

> *(***BIB*** *takes a treat from* ***JUNE*** *but then drops it on the ground.)*

JUNE. Oh, you're not hungry, Mama? Come here.

> *(***JUNE*** *pets* ***BIB****'s head and looks into her eyes.)*

I know you're tired girl. I am too. I. Am. Too.

(*WEEZY steals the treat intended for* **BIB**.)

WEEZY. (*"Nanny nanny boo boo."*) Meh eh eh eh ehhh eh.

JUNE. (*To* **WEEZY**.) Weezy, get back!

(*To* **BIB**.) Bib, you need to kick her ass. I know you could! I know you could. Who's my Steve Austin? Who's my Stone Cold Steve Austin?!

(**BIB** *turns to* **WEEZY** *and roars...*)

BIB. (*To* **WEEZY**.) MAAAAHHHH!!!!!!!!!!!!!

JUNE. Truth hurts, Weezy!

BIB. (*To* **WEEZY**.) MAAAAHHHH!!!!!!!!!!!!!

JUNE. (*Overlapping.*) Hell yeah!

(*To* **BIB**.) I am so proud of you, you want me to come out there? Lemme come out there.

(**JUNE** *turns to exit.*)

(*To* **ALICE**.) You're stayin for supper!

(**JUNE** *exits.*)

(*Calling from off.*)

Come on, Alice!

(**ALICE** *begins changing the lens on her camera.*)

(**ALICE**'s *muffled phone rings inside her bag, playing the same VERY UNPLEASANT RINGTONE.*)

(**ALICE** *dismisses the call and puts the cell phone in her pcoket.*)

WEEZY. (*To* **ALICE**. *Instructing.*) Nope.

(*Without skipping a beat,* **ALICE** *takes the phone back out of her pocket and returns it to her backpack.*)

(*She exits.*)

Scene Two

*(As before. Early evening. **WEEZY** looks on as **BIB** sleeps next to her on the pallet. **ALICE** looks through **JUNE**'s paintings. **JUNE** eats grapes from a colander and fiddles with **ALICE**'s camera.)*

JUNE. This isn't like any camera I remember.

ALICE. *(Demonstrating.)* It's like this.

JUNE. Oh, the button, got it, got it.

*(**JUNE** scrolls through the photographs on **ALICE**'s camera. Projection: The set becomes a living canvas. Image fragments, color, light, and texture, now filter in and out.)*

Oh, you got 'em both together, Bib's like, "What are you doin, weird new person?" Oh, look what you did, how do you do that? Even Weezy has that sad look, but not *sad* sad, more like, "I've seen things."

(Another photograph.)

Oh, there's another one, look at that, you should be a photographer.

(Another photograph.)

And Bib, look how cute, with her sneaky side eye, I love that. These are so good, Alice.

*(**JUNE** continues to scroll through photos.)*

(She freezes.)

*(**ALICE** walks over to the bed and looks at the viewfinder to see what **JUNE** is staring at.)*

ALICE. *Daniela.*

JUNE. Cancer?

ALICE. She chose not to have the reconstruction.

JUNE. Badass...

ALICE. Stage four. She won't live to see the book.

*(**JUNE** scrolls. Another woman.)*

Eve.

JUNE. Oh, my God...

ALICE. She was scalded as an infant. Her brother was supposed to give her a bath, but he forgot to check the water.

JUNE. How old was she?

ALICE. Ten months.

*(**JUNE** scrolls. Another woman.)*

*(Off **JUNE**'s reaction.)* Yeah...

(Beat.)

Nadja*.

JUNE. Nadja...

ALICE. Her husband threw acid in her face.

*(**JUNE** scrolls through the pictures of Nadja.)*

Pakistan. Her whole family shunned her. So she got out, escaped across the border. Got asylum.

JUNE. *Asylum.*

ALICE. She lives in Jersey now with her cousin.

*(**ALICE** pulls a book out of her backpack entitled* Breathe *and hands it to* **JUNE**.*)*

I met her when I was in rehab. She's teaching people how to stop crying.

*(**JUNE** takes the book and reads the back cover.)*

JUNE. How's that goin?

ALICE. I talked to her after the meeting. Told her about Chrissy. She knew the things to say.

JUNE. Chrissy...

(Beat.)

Y'all were together a long time?

---

* Pronounced "na-ja."

(**ALICE** *nods.*)

ALICE. Her parents were devastated. My dad...not so much.

JUNE. They didn't get along?

ALICE. "Dodged a bullet there, thank God the baby died with her."

JUNE. Oh, my God.

ALICE. "Why would you want to waste money on a second coffin, just bury them together."

(*Beat.*)

He doesn't want to actually see me. He just wants to see himself and his grand design staring back at him.

JUNE. I mean – it's not for me to say, but I would have kept them together.

ALICE. I did. But that's not the point.

JUNE. What is the point, that he has opinions? He's your daddy, he calls you, what, three times a day? He's tryin.

ALICE. He thinks I've gone crazy.

JUNE. How?

ALICE. Everything I've ever done has been tied to the family brand, I'm like the Anne Geddes of Hollywood cokeheads. You do one thing different and everyone freaks the fuck out.

JUNE. But you're doin *this* now.

ALICE. Yeah.

JUNE. It matters. Alice.

ALICE. Yeah.

JUNE. So tell him that.

(*Beat.*)

Do you miss him?

(*Beat.*)

So pick up the phone.

ALICE. I can't.

JUNE. Why not?

ALICE. It's too hard.

JUNE. Harder than *death*?

> *(Beat.)*

You lost a whole family.

ALICE. Question.

JUNE. Go.

ALICE. If someone said to you, "I have this magic memory-erasing pill, it can take back the part about your unborn baby, just one little pill and it will all go away," would you do it?

JUNE. No.

ALICE. Why not?

JUNE. Because I would want it to hurt.

> *(Beat.)*

You're supposed to hurt when you lose a child.

ALICE. Yeah, but...your brain would never know that you knew, it wouldn't know that you wanted to erase that memory, it wouldn't know anything, the memory would be gone.

JUNE. True. And... I still wouldn't want to be the kind of person that would say yes to an offer like that. It's my *child*.

> *(Beat.)*

Where do these people, like – like these idiots who try to talk to women after they miscarry, "Well, at least you can try again," like sayin, "It's not like you actually knew him or anything," FUCK YOU, that's my child! Takin a pill...it would be like killin him all over again. Or worse than death, to be forgotten.

> *(Beat.)*

I'll keep my memories, thank you very much.

> *(Pause.)*

Question?

ALICE. Go.

JUNE. So – why, after all that, would you –

WEEZY. *(Mostly to **JUNE**.)* "Why" is such a useless question.

JUNE. Why not landscapes? Polar bears?

WEEZY. *(Mostly to **JUNE**.)* What you're really askin is...

JUNE.	**WEEZY**.
*(To **ALICE**.)*	*(To **ALICE** – continuous.)*
How bad did it get?	"How bad did it get?"

> (**WEEZY** *has now entered **ALICE**'s orbit. She addresses nearly all her comments to **ALICE** and **JUNE**, with an occasional line tossed in the direction of the audience (note: this is not a "Ted Talk" – it should not, in any way, sound like a lecture or a morality tale.)*

> (**WEEZY** *stays close.* **ALICE**, *still unable to actually hear **WEEZY**, may now begin to notice a gentle disturbance in "The Force," but pushes through...)*

ALICE. I didn't work for a long time after the accident.

WEEZY. Like a *really* long time.

ALICE. I just couldn't get my footing.

WEEZY. Two bottles a day.

ALICE. And then there was rehab.

WEEZY. Three failed rehabs. Two DUIs and a night in the county jail.

ALICE. I lost a few days.

WEEZY. But the mug shot was *amaaaaazing,* am I right?

> (**ALICE** *recalls the mug shot (it really was amazing). She tries to shake it off.)*

Selective editing. Because *art,* because *shame,* because *dissonance,* because *romanticizin the pain,* because if I give you the full crazy you will run very, very fast in all of the opposite directions.

> *(Beat.)*

What we leave out.

ALICE. And then...

WEEZY. What we leave in...

ALICE. *(As if drawing a breath of fresh air.)* I met Nadja. And she invited me over for lunch. And I told her all about Chrissy and the baby and my stupid dad. And she just kept *pouring the tea*. She was wearing this gorgeous copper sari...and I'm sitting across from this creature and this *feast* she called lunch. The life from this woman, the heat from her heart was like the pull of gravity. It was like, I wanted to know her pain. To *mix it in with mine*. To tell her how grateful I was that she...

>   *(Beat.)*

We sat there in the quiet. And she put her hand on mine and asked me to take her picture. All our dishes were still sitting around, and I didn't change a thing, I thought...this looks like love to me. I don't remember a single frame, I was shaking and the lens kept blurring over and she finally just grabbed me and pulled me in. And I could smell her hair...and her skin was like –

>   *(Beat.)*

I sobbed and sobbed.

>   *(Beat.)*

I don't want to forget.

JUNE. Well, then you won't.

>   *(Pause.)*

ALICE. I'm supposed to drive to Atlanta tomorrow.

>   *(Beat.)*

JUNE. *Tomorrow.*

ALICE. Yeah. Have you been?

JUNE. Little kid. School trip.

>   *(Beat.)*

What's her name?

ALICE. Nell.

JUNE. What happened to Nell?

ALICE. You don't want to know.

JUNE. I do.

> *(Pause.)*

ALICE. She was...raped by her uncle when she was nine years old. And then the next day when she threatened to tell her mother, he punched her in the head until she could no longer see.

JUNE. Oh...

ALICE. She's fifty-three years old now. She teaches piano to little kids. And she's *happy*.

> (**ALICE** *picks up the painting of the cat.*)

Why don't you want people to see your work?

JUNE. *(Instantly agitated.)* Would you like a grape?

ALICE. No, thank you.

JUNE. You sure?

ALICE. I'm sure.

JUNE. They're really good.

> *(Begin rapid fire.)*

(Words tumbling.) I can't stop. It's my internet, it's my porn, it's my / whatever, it's ridiculous. Have a grape.

> (**JUNE** *tries handing* **ALICE** *a handful of grapes.*)

JUNE.	ALICE.
(Continuous.) If I stop I die, have a grape.	Can't stop.
HAVE A GRAPE, HAVE A FUCKING GRAPE.	I don't want –

> (**ALICE** *reluctantly take a grape.*)

ALICE. These must be really good grapes...

JUNE. You have NO IDEA!

> *(Beat.)*

ALICE. Question.

JUNE. No.

ALICE. Question.

JUNE. NO.

ALICE. You really don't want me doing this do you?

JUNE. You're a damn genius!

WEEZY. *(To* **JUNE.***)* Oh my God!

>   (**WEEZY** *enters* **JUNE***'s orbit now.)*
>
>   *(End rapid fire.)*

ALICE.
(To **JUNE.***)* What's the point of all this, if no one will ever see it?

JUNE.
(To **ALICE.***)* You think I'm lookin for approval?

WEEZY.
(To **JUNE.***)* Did you really not see this coming June, you bring a world famous photographer into your house

why would she have any questions, June, WHY WOULD SHE HAVE ANY QUESTIONS?

>   *(Beat.)*

ALICE. Art is meant to be shared.

JUNE. *Art is meant to be shared?* You sound like a really bad greetin card and not like Hallmark, like Dollar General. *Meant to be shared.* That's not a rule, Alice, and if it was, I'd kick its ugly face in.

ALICE. Wow.

JUNE. I don't need to share. I don't need to do anything except what I'm doin.

WEEZY. *(To* **JUNE.***)* Because it's workin out so well.

ALICE. You know what I've noticed?

JUNE. I would *love* to know!

ALICE. Every time we talk about your work, you get *hostile.* It's almost as if you don't want us to talk about your work. And I think it's you, JUNE, truthfully, you don't want the world to see you.

JUNE. *(Regarding the painting* **ALICE** *is holding.)* Upside down.

> *(***ALICE** *turns the painting right side up.)*

ALICE. You use a lot of wood.

JUNE. Barn scraps.

ALICE. Why wood? Why not...canvas?

JUNE. This feels weird.

ALICE. It does?

JUNE. It feels like I'm angry with you and you're askin me these questions, and I'd rather not be a fuckin bitch when I answer them.

ALICE. I told you *my* story...

> *(Pause.)*

JUNE. *(Softening.)* Yeah. Yeah, you did...

> *(***JUNE** *looks to* **WEEZY** *for a "power-up," a shot of courage. They lock eyes. Power is exchanged.* **JUNE** *and* **WEEZY** *take a deep breath in unison.)*

(To **ALICE** *– stepping in...)* Canvas doesn't...feel as good. There's no *history*. Wood is unpredictable. It's... never the same two pieces, and it's, it's got flaws and inclusions and dirt and stuff and I get it to tell me what it wants to be and we have a conversation.

> *(Beat.)*

I was in a wheelchair when I painted that one. That's how it started. Physical therapy. She wanted me to...*do* things. So I did a thing. And then I did another thing. That was my third paintin, actually.

> *(Beat.)*

I hate the world and I'm in it.

> *(***JUNE** *looks at the video camera and up at* **ALICE. ALICE** *gives* **JUNE** *an "Are you sure?" look.* **JUNE** *nods.)*

You can't undo things and you can't –

(**ALICE** *turns on the camera.* **WEEZY** *watches intently.*)

(**JUNE** *begins.*)

Mama was up late doin laundry, same as always, just got home from a double at the hospital and she was so tired, so I went and fed Amy and tucked her in.

ALICE. Your daughter.

JUNE. My sister. Baby sister. She wanted me to sing to her. I remember her smilin up at me, blinkin those pretty eyes, like, "I'm not sleepy," but she was fightin. I said *little girl, you will not win, I will sing you down and you will not win.* She fought so hard. But she finally fell asleep with her little rag doll and I passed out in the rocker.

(*Beat.*)

It came in the night. It was so weird. I woke up thinkin *has Mama turned on the attic fan,* all the air was movin from the room and Amy yellin, "Train, it's a train, Jubee!" I looked up and the window was gone, like fuckin gone. And then it was black, everything was black, I could hear Mama callin from the porch, and little Amy was screamin her head off, "Jubee, Jubee," reachin for me.

(*Beat.*)

I snatched her up, ran to the porch, and Mama yellin, "Get in the cellar!" I ran around to the side yard and grabbed ahold of the cellar door and it ripped away from me, right outta my hands, right offa the hinges, knocked me back. Holdin on to Amy so tight, and Mama screamin, "Where's Daddy?" It was all I could do to hold on to Amy, she was – she was so scared, she was callin for the cat, "Where's Pekoe? Where's Pekoe," and the rain, God the rain, and the noise, I couldn't hear a thing, I looked up to see a flash of white headed into the barn, maybe a hundred yards, but I knew it was Daddy. Seein about the horses. I called to him…

(Pause.)

And then it came. And it was around us, the most sickenin sound I have ever heard, and it was like God had reached down and twisted off a piece of the Earth. And then *nothin*...for like...*whole seconds.*

(Beat.)

It was the barn. With Daddy in it. It was gone. It was there and then it was gone. I couldn't get into the cellar...there was nothin to grab hold of, and then the porch broke sideways, right offa the house, and Amy still hollerin for Pekoe and Mama screamin, "The porch, the porch!"

(Pause.)

You try to tell people what it feels like...when a barn and *half a house* rains down on top of you. It's not a *storm.* It's not an *accident. It's three point two seconds* and it's a *thousand rusty knives* before you have time to pray, and then it's pushin you down into the *cold red mud* and the world is gone and *I'm dead, this is it.*

(Beat.)

But that wasn't even the worst part. Lyin there in the dark and this sound, this *awful* sound, so loud, and it's over and over, and its not stoppin, like a hammer, and it's louder and louder, and it's findin out it's my own *chest* and whatever's left inside tryin to *chew its way out with its teeth.* And then Amy's sweet little voice. So soft and still, like she was talkin in her sleep, and she was so far away – how did she get so far away?

(Amy's voice.) "Where's Pekoe? Where's Pekoe?"

All gone...

*(**ALICE** looks at the painting.)*

ALICE. That's Pekoe?

(Beat.)

God...

(**JUNE** *begins digging in the hope chest for sheets and pillow cases.*)

JUNE. I'm 'on get you some sheets, set you up in the spare room.

(*Beat.*)

I lost two months. I don't know where they went, I woke up and everybody was runnin around tryin not to tell me what they needed to tell me. I broke my neck. Both legs. My skin was sliced open in thirty-two places. Seven months, eight surgeries and twelve more scars to show for it.

ALICE. Your family…

JUNE. They're all buried here. When I finally got home, all the mess was cleared away and there were markers out at the edge of the pasture.

(*Holding up some bedding options.*)

You like a pink sheet or a flannel, too hot for flannel…

(*Beat.*)

I planted berries and butterfly bush so they wouldn't be lonely. And that's my sad story.

ALICE. Why did you come back here?

JUNE. Is there somewhere else? I get up every day and I clean the coop and I get the eggs and I feed the goats and I make a sandwich and that's my life. That's my life.

(**ALICE** *turns off the video camera.*)

ALICE. Thank you.

JUNE. Sure.

(*Calmly. Curiously.*) There's somethin in my hair…

ALICE. What?

JUNE. (*Only slightly annoyed by the bug.*) I don't know, get it.

(**ALICE** *goes to inspect.*)

I'm like some kind of garden witch. Never mind, I got it.

(**JUNE** *pulls a ladybug out of her hair.*)

ALICE. It's a ladybug.

JUNE. They live in there, and click beetles and God knows what else, s'what I get for sleepin with the windows open.

ALICE. Those are good luck, ya know, you gotta make a wish.

(**JUNE** *goes to the window. She closes her eyes, makes a wish, and then blows the ladybug out of the window as if blowing out a birthday candle.* **WEEZY** *smiles tenderly at* **JUNE**. *The ladybug flutters all around* **BIB** *who delights in the little visitor. Everyone watches as it entertains* **BIB** *for a moment and then flutters off.*)

JUNE. *(To the ladybug.)* Good luck, ladybug. With your ladybug girlfriend. At the ladybug picnic.

(*Pause.*)

(*Breathing in the fresh air.*)

I want to go to Mexico.

ALICE. You're not supposed to tell me your wish!

JUNE. No, that's not my wish, I just wanna go to Mexico. We were supposed to go as a family.

(**JUNE** *goes to her cabinet and pulls out a few travel books and hands them to* **ALICE**.)

ALICE. Oh?

JUNE. Daddy had it all mapped out.

ALICE. You were close?

(**JUNE** *nods. During the following,* **JUNE** *pulls out a box of travel books, maps, etc., and sits on the bed to sift through it.* **ALICE** *eventually joins her on the bed.*)

There's tickets in here. *Somewhere.* He was really good at planning.

> *(Beat.)*

The things you never get around to.

> *(**ALICE** picks up a travel book.)*

ALICE. Todos Santos...

JUNE. You know it?

ALICE. I've been there. Twice.

JUNE. Really?

ALICE. Mountains...ocean. A lot of artists go there. You could go there and paint.

JUNE. What did you want to be when you were growin up, a photographer?

> *(During the following, **ALICE**'s focus is on a big fold-out map of Todos Santos.)*

ALICE. I used to sneak into Dad's darkroom. Open up the boxes and breathe in the smells, you know how film has that smell? He showed me how to see things. And then one day something came in the mail. Dad said, go ahead, open it. His picture was on the cover of *Vogue* magazine. And then I turn to see my dad just beaming from the kitchen. And he's standing there in nothing but a white oxford shirt and black socks, smoking a cigar with Lauren Hutton. "Howdayah like me now, kid?" Except I didn't know it was Lauren Hutton. Or any of them, actually. They were just *pretty ladies* who hung around and brought me chocolates.

JUNE. Your mama must have hated that.

ALICE. She was gone by then.

> *(Off **JUNE**'s look.)*

Breast cancer.

> *(**JUNE** reaches over to touch **ALICE**'s bracelet. **ALICE** reacts to the warmth of **JUNE**'s hand.)*

JUNE. So, you knew Chrissy was pregnant before she left for Vermont, right?

    (Beat.)

So, why didn't you go with her?

ALICE. *Work.*

JUNE. That's gotta be super fucked up. You wouldn't be lyin here with me right now.

ALICE. I've thought about it. Or maybe we'd have gone a different route. Like West through Albany. Along the river.

JUNE. I should have left her in her bed.

ALICE. Don't do that.

JUNE. Oh, I'm doin it.

    (Pause.)

What do you ache for, Alice?

    (A very long pause.)

ALICE. To be seen?

    *(**JUNE** nods.)*

(Regarding Mexico.) You can still go, ya know?

JUNE. *(Deflecting.)* Are you gettin hungry?

ALICE. June.

JUNE. *(Avoiding.)* I got some purple hulls comin in out back, some early okra.

    (Beat.)

ALICE. I spent three months on a sofa out in Long Island. I didn't leave the house for fifty-seven days.

JUNE. Nine hundred forty-five.

    (Beat.)

ALICE. What?

JUNE. Nine hundred forty-five days. I think we have some turnips too. Tomatoes and cukes, let's go out back.

ALICE. Nine hundred forty-five –

JUNE. *(Overlapping.)* I'm the next Harper Lee.

ALICE. How do you manage?

JUNE. Umm, I manage.

ALICE. Do you –

JUNE. *(Continuous.)* For the most part. I know some VERY GOOD enablers. So.

> *(Beat.)*

I mean, I don't like it, it's not my first ch – you're totally freakin out right now, shit, let me go cut up some okra.

> *(**JUNE** looks for her shoes.)*

ALICE. June.

JUNE. *(Words tumbling.)* You know that thing where you show up to a blind date and dude is standin there with one leg? I got one leg, Alice. One leg.

ALICE. You have two. I don't like okra.

> *(All action stops as **JUNE**, **WEEZY**, and finally **BIB** all turn to glare at **ALICE**.)*

JUNE. *(Deadly serious.)* What did you say?

ALICE. I don't like okra.

> *(Beat.)*

JUNE. *(Aghast.)* YOU SHUT YOUR MOUTH get outta this house.

ALICE. Slimy. Gross.

JUNE. That's not on the okra, Alice, that is not the okra's fault.

ALICE. Snails on a plate.

JUNE. *(Overlapping.)* Who the fuck has been feedin you?

> *(Beat.)*

ALICE. *(Needling.)* Cracker Barrel.

JUNE. *(Practically hissing.)*	**WEEZY.** *(Spitting mad.)*
NOT FUNNY. NOT FUNNY. NOT FUNNY.	Pffff! Pffff! BE-Pffff!

ALICE. We were talking about Mexico. It's a two hour plane ride from here. And I / bet they have okra.

>(**JUNE** *exits.*)

JUNE. *(Overlapping. Exiting.)* You need to put your *flip flops* ON and MEET ME OUT BACK!

ALICE. *(Overlapping, calling.)* How bad is it?

>(*Beat.*)

Can you get into town? The crossing?

>(**JUNE** *re-enters.*)

The mailbox?

JUNE. I can get to the crossin, I just can't –

>(*She does a "crossing over" gesture.*)

Peachy's house. And her barn, just barely.

ALICE. And then what?

JUNE. Outer space. Oxygen free.

ALICE. Nine hundred forty-five days?

JUNE. *(Deflecting, words tumbling.)* There was a boy in my tenth grade history class, I remember him sayin some stupid shit about Mexicans, like how they should get their own country and stay off our beaches. I said you are one stupid motherfucker, you know that? I was like *dude, you do realize we share the same beach, right? Like... It's the Gulf of Mexico, not the Gulf of Fuckin Dipshit Alabama.*

ALICE. *(Concerned.)* June?

JUNE. *(Anxious.)* I'm not ready. Ya know?

ALICE. I do.

JUNE. *(Brightly.)* So, I'll meet you out back then?

ALICE. Sure.

>(**JUNE** *exits.*)

Scene Three

(Moments later.)

*(***WEEZY*** *enters the garden area and digs up a mason jar filled with pickled okra. She opens it and starts snacking.* ***JUNE*** *enters and begins picking vegetables.)*

JUNE. Why do you eat the okra, I give you carrots.

WEEZY. This isn't about the okra.

*(***ALICE*** *emerges onto the porch and looks out at the pasture. She takes a few pictures.* ***WEEZY*** *watches her intently.)*

I don't like carrots...

JUNE. You're a goat, goats eat everything.

WEEZY. *(Regarding* ***ALICE**.*) I like her, she's unafraid.

JUNE. *(Preemptively.)* Stop. Go do your goat things.

WEEZY. *(Amused.)* Really? *Goat things?*

JUNE. Fuck off. How 'bout that?

(Beat.)

*(***WEEZY*** *catches* ***JUNE*** *looking over at* ***ALICE**.*)

WEEZY. *(Amused.)* Are you blushin?

JUNE. Shut up.

*(***BIB*** *moves, adjusts, falls back asleep.)*

WEEZY. *(Regarding* ***BIB**.*) Soon.

JUNE. I'll call the vet.

WEEZY. No. She doesn't want all that. She just wants to go.

(Pause.)

(Guardedly.) When she dies, I'm 'on take off.

JUNE. For how long?

(Pause.)

(Off ***WEEZY**'s *look.)* Oh.

(Stung.) I hadn't realized I was so impossible.

WEEZY. S'OK, I realized it enough for the both of us.

>   *(Beat.)*

I gotta do some things.

JUNE. Like what?

WEEZY. *(Needling.) Goat things.*
(Tenderly.) She wanted me to tell you she's sorry for
eatin up all your okra.

JUNE. She said that?

WEEZY. No.

>   *(Pause.)*

JUNE. I don't want you to go.

>   *(JUNE walks over to BIB and kisses her on the
>   head.)*

Oh, sweet Bib. I'm so sorry, Weezy.

WEEZY. Hey, you know me. I always land on my feet.
Hooves.

>   *(JUNE exits. WEEZY watches ALICE for a
>   moment and then turns her attention to BIB.)*

>   *(Lights fade as WEEZY leads BIB offstage.
>   Lights up on JUNE's room.)*

Scene Four

*(**JUNE**'s bedroom. Two a.m. A wind chime is heard chattering away outside.)*

*(**JUNE** enters her room and climbs into bed (which may or may not still be covered with a pile of maps and books). She drifts off to sleep...)*

*(A bolt of lightning followed immediately by a loud thunder crack. **JUNE** bolts upright in bed, terrified and hysterical. She springs into action.)*

JUNE. Fuck!

(A cacophony of noise, flashes of lightning, pounding thunder and the sound of a fast moving freight train, horns blaring, wood cracking.)

Shoes! Shoes! Shoes!

*(**JUNE** puts on her shoes.)*

(The sound of ripping metal.)

Oh, fuck.

(She gathers items...)

Pillows! Flash light. In the tub, everything in the tub. Shit.

(She throws all the items into a pile near the door and then goes for the mattress. She tries to drag it off the bed...)

(Yanking at the mattress.)

Gotta go. Gotta go.

(Sound of Amy crying, "Jubee! Jubee!")

Amy. Amy??

(Air raid siren.)

(JUNE runs to the door, but it won't open.)

AMY!!! AMY!!!!!!!!!!!! OH MY GOD...

(She pulls on it, over and over but it won't budge. Amy's cries continue...)

(Ad lib.) AMY!!!!! AMY!!! WHERE ARE YOU?!!!

(JUNE pounds on the door. She runs to the window and opens it. The wind and rain rush in, pushing her back. She tries to reach the window again, but it's no use. Another loud punch of noise and then a great swooping vacuum of silence followed by an explosion as the world goes black.)

Oh my God, oh my God, oh my God, Amy!!!

(WEEZY enters the light. Perhaps she has conjured this "storm" or perhaps not. She is invested in the outcome and watches on intently.)

(The door to the bedroom opens and ALICE rushes in just as JUNE reaches the window.)

JUNE. *(Screaming out the window.)* Amy! Where are you???!

ALICE. June!

JUNE. Amy!!!!!!!!!

(ALICE pulls JUNE back from the window and slams it shut.)

(The noise continues.)

ALICE. June!

JUNE. No, no, no, no, no! AMY!!!!

ALICE. June, it's OK, you awake? Wake up, June!

JUNE. I'm gonna fuckin die here!

ALICE. Wake up, babe.

JUNE. Oh, my God, Amy!

ALICE. Wake up, June. Wake up for me.

JUNE. Amy. Amy. Amy. Amy. Amy. Amy. Amy. Amy.

ALICE. *(Shaking* **JUNE.***)* JUNE! JUNE!!!!

> *(Clap of thunder.)*

> *(***JUNE** *startles with a violent inhale of air, as if surfacing from deep water.)*

> *(***ALICE** *catches sight of* **WEEZY** *exiting into the darkness.)*

> *(***JUNE** *looks around, wide-eyed and bewildered.)*

(Softly.) Holy shit. Are you OK?

JUNE. Fuuuuuck...

> *(***JUNE** *stares at* **ALICE.***)*

> *(Thunder rips fast across the dark night sky.)*

> *(***JUNE** *pulls* **ALICE** *into her clutches.)*

> *(The rain follows, a thrashing torrent on tin roof.)*

> *(They melt into the bed.)*

> *(Lights fade.)*

End of Act I

A NOTE ABOUT THE INTIMACY
AT THE END OF ACT I

In terms of whether or not June and Alice "sleep together" at the end of Act I – i.e., whether the physicality in the final moments is platonic, innocent, suggested, explicit – I'm intentionally leaving that open to interpretation.

While I would agree that intimacy is a singular experience and that writers are encouraged to be *specific* with their ideas, I have always approached my work pragmatically and encourage interpreters of my work to do the same. So, out of respect for each theater and their individual needs, I do not wish to constrain or require any specific degree of physicality, nudity, etc.

You have my blessing to work with your actors to find what feels right for you and for your unique audiences. Any allusions found in the remainder of the text regarding the physical nature of Alice and June's relationship should *work* regardless of how you choose to "end" Act I.

My advice would be to decide (through experimentation) the degree of mystery and innocence you'd like to see throughout the play and work your way "back" from there. If there *is* to be anything beyond just a platonic moment, June should be the one to initiate. If that is the case, then I might recommend Alice pull back at first, in an effort to protect June. I leave the rest up to you.

ACT II

Scene One

(Sunday. Early morning.)

(Lights up on **JUNE** *in her room sitting on her bed, reading Nadja's book.)*

(Outside, **ALICE** *is in the yard on a yoga mat finishing up her daily yoga routine.* **BIB** *sleeps on her pallet.* **WEEZY** *sits on the porch with her lunch, a Red Bull and a big salad in a carry-out container. She eats her salad with a spork and watches* **ALICE**.*)*

ALICE. Just gonna sit over there and watch, I guess.

(Beat.)

Different kinda goat yoga.

(Beat.)

Passive aggressive goat yoga… hashtag *goat shit*, hashtag *YOLO. (Ad lib.)*

WEEZY. *(Overlapping.)* Nice form.

ALICE. *(Reflexively.)* Thanks.

(Beat.)

Oh God.

*(***WEEZY** *waves her spork in greeting. She resumes eating.)*

(Long pause as **ALICE** *tries to process how to respond to a talking goat.)*

59

Did you just –

    (Pause.)

Are – are you eating a salad?

WEEZY. *Couscous.*

    *(**WEEZY** continues to eat. **ALICE** steps in cautiously...)*

ALICE. Couscous? Interesting.

    (Beat.)

I, umm... I used to be... afraid of couscous...

WEEZY. Is that right?

ALICE. Yeah, actually. When I was little.

    *(**WEEZY** stares directly at **ALICE** and awaits an explanation.)*

The, uh...

WEEZY. Use your words.

ALICE. The, uh...right, umm, when I was twelve years old it was on the menu at my summer camp a coupla times, and then one day Tommy Fitzpatrick told everyone in the lunch room that couscous was made out of eyeballs.

    *(**WEEZY** pauses with a mouth full of food.)*

*(Off **WEEZY**'s look. Tentatively.)* So. As you can imagine –

WEEZY. *(Overlapping.)* What kind of eyeballs?

    (Pause.)

ALICE. *(Sheepishly.)* Sheep?

    *(**WEEZY** suddenly loses her appetite.)*

    *(**ALICE** resumes her yoga but her focus remains on **WEEZY**.)*

What are you?

WEEZY. I'm some kind of like wise Yoda, gouda, kinda thing, you should ask the author.

ALICE. Yoda...

WEEZY. *(Brusquely.)* Are you 'bout done with the *salute the sun dog-facin*, I need you to do somethin for me.

>*(Instructing.)*

In the grass there is a gold cross. You're supposed to put it in your pocket and give it to June at a pivotal moment in the story so she can have an emotional reaction to it.

ALICE. *(Searching.)* Over here?

WEEZY. Up under yer wee wee pad.

ALICE. My what?

WEEZY. The pad, the mattress pad!

ALICE. Oh.

>*(**ALICE** lifts up her yoga mat and sees the necklace immediately.)*

Oh, I see it.

>*(**ALICE** picks up the necklace and examines it.)*

WEEZY. *(All business.)* Now listen, that belonged to Miss Elsee, June's mama. She was a preacher's wife and he gave it to her on their weddin night. She never took it off, not once in all those years.

ALICE.	**WEEZY**.
OK.	*(Brusquely.)* Put it in your pocket.
Wow.	
I don't have a pocket.	Yeah you do.

ALICE. *(Fucking <u>delighted</u> to find a pocket.)* I *do* have a pocket!!!

(Appreciatively.) What?! I never use that pocket!!!

WEEZY. *(Dryly.)* It's what I do.

>*(Pause.)*

ALICE. You seem grumpy.

>*(Pause.)*

WEEZY. *(Flatly.)* I seem grumpy?

> *(Begin rapid fire.)*

ALICE. Yes.

WEEZY. Was Yoda grumpy?

ALICE. Yes.

WEEZY. Gandalf?

ALICE. Yes.

WEEZY. Mr. Miy-ag-i?

> *(**WEEZY** pulls herself up into a* Karate Kid *crane pose...)*

ALICE. *(Overlapping – amused.)* Fine.

> *(End rapid fire. Pause.)*

WEEZY. You want the truth?

ALICE. *(Stepping lightly.)* Yes, I wanna say yes?

WEEZY. I'm tired of lookin after everybody.

> *(Beat.)*

I'm tired in general.

> *(**ALICE** locks eyes with **WEEZY**. After a moment...)*

Does it work?

ALICE. Yes.

> *(**WEEZY** gestures for **ALICE** to resume her yoga. She watches on for a bit and then, unseen by **ALICE**, **WEEZY** slowly pretzels her body into a hilarious and spectacularly impossible yoga position.)*

WEEZY. *(Maneuvering.)* What does it do?

ALICE. It feels amazing. And when I'm done I can almost breathe, almost.

> *(**ALICE** turns to see **WEEZY** nearly upside-down.)*

(Amused.) You wanna try?

WEEZY. Nope.

ALICE. You sure?

WEEZY. *(Covering as if inspecting a porch board or a patch of fescue.)* Yep.
(Ad lib.) That's a good board right there. *Solid.*

> *(Inside the house, we see* **JUNE** *putting the book away and pulling out some art supplies and an old quilt.)*

> *(***BIB** *awakens to a twisting pain. She cries out. Her blanket falls loose.)*

Okay, mama, okay!

> *(***ALICE** *pauses her yoga to watch on as* **WEEZY** *cares for* **BIB**.*)*

> *(***WEEZY** *comforts her mother through the wave of pain.* **BIB** *cries out again.* **ALICE** *watches on, concerned.)*

> *(Pause.)*

WEEZY. *(To* **ALICE**.*)* Do you miss her?

> *(***ALICE** *stares at* **WEEZY**…*astonished to learn that she knows about Chrissy.)*

ALICE. Every day.

> *(Beat.)*

Every hour.

WEEZY. What do you miss most?

> *(No response from* **ALICE**. **WEEZY** *turns to look at her.)*

ALICE. That's so weird.

WEEZY. What?

ALICE. She's been gone almost a year now and that is the first time anyone has asked me that question.

WEEZY. *(Tenderly.)* Well, I'm asking.

(**BIB** *sighs a contented sigh.* **ALICE** *and* **WEEZY** *now watch over* **BIB** *who has fallen back asleep.*)

ALICE. Her laugh. They way she would sing, show tunes, just whatever, sing for any reason, any place, full volume – I'm talking to a goat.

WEEZY. Shit. Like right now?

(*Beat.*)

That's fucked up.

(**ALICE** *and* **WEEZY** *look on as* **JUNE** *appears at an open window and shakes out the quilt.*)

It's on *you* now. You know that, right?

(**JUNE** *turns on her little portable radio. A joyful music* * *fills the entire scene, as:*)

(**WEEZY** *tucks* **BIB** *in and begins fixing one of the unruly braids in her mother's hair.* **ALICE** *resumes her yoga routine.*)

(*The music is now at full volume as the focus turns to* **JUNE**...)

(**JUNE** *finds* **ALICE**'s *shirt among the covers. She holds it for a moment, taking it in, and then places it off to the side. She puts the old quilt on her bed to catch the paint and dirt and then sits on her bed with a painting in progress. She selects her paint and readies her brush. She begins.*)

(**ALICE** *finishes her yoga routine and exits.*)

(**WEEZY** *finishes up with her mother's hair and sits nearby in the lawn chair.*)

---

* A license to produce *Alabaster* does not include a performance license for any third-party or copyrighted music. Licensees should create an original composition or use music in the public domain. For further information, please see Music Use Note on page 3.

> (**ALICE** *enters* **JUNE**'s *room.* **JUNE** *turns off the radio and continues to paint. She does not make eye contact.*)

JUNE. Hey, what's good?

ALICE. I was just, uh, outside talking to your goat.

JUNE. Is she givin you a hard time?

ALICE. A little, yeah – also, I was just *outside.* Talking to a *goat.*

JUNE. It's catching.

ALICE. Uh huh.

JUNE. She's like *plague. Black death.*

> (**ALICE** *retrieves her shirt and puts it with her belongings.* **JUNE** *notices.*)

ALICE. *(Off* **JUNE**'s *look.)* You OK?

JUNE. Sure.

ALICE. This word, "sure," does it really mean sure?

JUNE. Sure.

> (**ALICE** *notices the painting.*)

ALICE. *(Hesitantly.)* That's a little different than your usual fare…

> *(Beat.)*

Lovers?

JUNE. Maybe.

ALICE. Maybe.

JUNE. *(Coldly.)* Maybe they're just strangers who fuck.

ALICE. *(Stung.)* No harm in it.

JUNE. Nope.

ALICE. It's pretty.

JUNE. It's not done, hand me the yellow.

ALICE. *(Regarding the painting.)* Another barn scrap?

JUNE. *(Regarding the yellow paint.)* It's right over there.

> (**ALICE** *retrieves the yellow paint but then stops in her tracks. She looks at the piles of*

*wood in the room – really <u>seeing</u> them for the
first time.)*

(Long pause.)

ALICE. *(Apprehensively.)* June? Where do you get the barn
scraps you use in your paintings?

JUNE. From the barn, duh.

ALICE. You don't have a barn.

> (**ALICE** *looks around the room again,
> finally understanding the scope of* **JUNE***'s
> compulsion.)*

> *(Long pause.)*

Are you telling me that all of this wood that you've been
painting on is from –

> *(Beat.)*

What happens when you run out of wood?

> *(Beat.)*

That was a serious question. / June?

JUNE. *(Overlapping – agitated.)* I'm happy when I'm
paintin.

ALICE. OK.

JUNE. There's no pain when I'm paintin.

ALICE. OK, I get that. It's just...there's so *much* of it, June.

> *(Beat.)*

This isn't healthy.

JUNE. *(Agitated.)* Hand me that towel, please.

> (**ALICE** *notices the agitation, she retrieves the
> towel and sits with* **JUNE**, *taking her hands in
> hers. They lock eyes.* **JUNE** *takes a deep breath.
> She settles.)*

I never saw them go into the ground. I always thought
when I buried my mother I'd be able to pick out her
dress. Nope. And Daddy would have *hated* to be buried
in the south pasture. He wanted to be cremated and

thrown into Pensacola Bay. And damnit, people oughta leave this world the way they want to!

(Beat.)

After I made that little garden, I came back two days later and all my lavender had been chewed up. I thought it was deer, but then I remembered they don't like lavender. So, I planted some more and then I found my binoculars and started watchin from the kitchen window. And then one day I saw her. It was that little shit Weezy. Eatin up all my lavender, butterfly bush. I ran out the back door, I've never run so fast. And she saw me and started runnin. I was like *where have you been,* honestly I really thought she was dead. She must have just been hangin out down by the crossin all that time, there's good water there.

ALICE. So, Weezy survived the storm?

JUNE. I don't know how.

ALICE. And Bib?

JUNE. That's Weezy's mama. I went up there and took her back from Mr. Autrey up the road so Weezy could have somebody. Don't laugh. I used to let her sleep with me. She'd lay there and I'd look into those big brown eyes and her lookin back at me. She's got the pain and lonely of the whole world inside her. Storm passes through, and she's wanderin around…all her friends and family…

(Beat.)

Once she found out I was back, she wouldn't leave me the hell alone.

WEEZY. *(Correcting.)* You wouldn't leave *me* alone.

JUNE. Scratchin at the window.

(Beat.)

I made a little bed for her in the corner, ya know, what the hell. And then I woke up and she had climbed into bed with me.

WEEZY. No, you *put* me in bed with you and it was somethin like a *choke* hold.

(JUNE talks with ALICE but her focus now turns to WEEZY.)

JUNE. We stayed like that for weeks. And then one day she didn't climb into bed like normal.

(Beat.)

And I realized I felt better. And I started thinkin that's what that was, she was takin the pain away, and I know how that sounds but why else would I just all of a sudden start feelin better on the *one day* she started sleepin back on the floor.

WEEZY. Because you wouldn't stop kickin me.

JUNE. And you fart in your sleep.

WEEZY. Well you would know, *fart queen*!

JUNE.	WEEZY.
Be *ashamed.* Be ashamed.	Olympic gold fart champion of the world.

JUNE. Shut up and be ashamed.

(To ALICE.) She farts in her sleep.

(Pause.)

ALICE. You know, June, I could sit here and tell you that your work deserves to be seen, and it does, and you don't want to hear it, and that's fine. But I'm talking about you, June. You're a beautiful, vibrant woman and you are meant for more than this. You've been alone for so long.

(Beat.)

Your parents...they wouldn't have wanted this for you.

JUNE. *(Agitated.)* I'm gonna get some iced tea, you want some?

ALICE. *(Impulsively.)* Come with me to Atlanta.

(JUNE glares at ALICE.)

(Decidedly.) Yeah. You should come.

JUNE. *(Dumbfounded.)* Why?

ALICE. Because it would be good for you.

(**JUNE** *looks at* **ALICE** *like a dog tilting its head at a far away noise.*)

JUNE. (*Slow and deliberate.*) OK... I'm really *thirsty*...right now. So, I'm gonna go and get some *iced tea*. Like people *do*. From the *kitchen*. Where it's *located*.

(**JUNE** *exits.*)

(**BIB**'s *breathing becomes labored.* **WEEZY** *cries out.*)

(*Bedroom:* **ALICE**, *hearing the goat sounds, looks around for the kibble and pours a cup full out the window.*)

(**ALICE**'s *phone rings, but this time with a more NEUTRAL RINGTONE. She answers it.*)

ALICE. Hey. How are you? Oh? Is it raining up there? Oh, good, I'm so out of it. No, it's good, I'm down here in Alabama. Feedin some goats. Yeah, like right outside Birmingham. Oh my God, you have no idea.

(**JUNE** *returns with two glasses of tea and stands in the doorway listening to* **ALICE**'s *phone call.*)

She's got these paintings, they're ridiculous[*], I can't even. I'll try to send you a picture. I'd love for you to meet her.

(**ALICE** *notices* **JUNE** *standing in the doorway.*)

I will. I think she'd like that, actually. OK. Oh, no, don't burn dinner. No, you go, I'll find you later. OK, babe. Bye.

JUNE.	ALICE.
You're tellin people about me?	
Alice?	June, I –

---

[*] Incredible.

JUNE.	ALICE.
I really wish you hadn't done that. Wrappin me up like some country bumpkin discovery. Who was that, your agent?	that was –

ALICE. I'll let you calm down.

JUNE. Calm down?

ALICE. See, this is exactly what I was getting / at. It's like you – ya know, what, I'm not gonna say it.

JUNE. *(Overlapping.)* I hate that you did that. HATE.

ALICE. What exactly is it you think I did just now?

JUNE. *(Overlapping.)* I don't want you tellin people about me.

JUNE.	ALICE.
I'm not for sale!	June.

ALICE. That wasn't my agent, June.

JUNE. I don't care who it was, you don't talk / about me.

ALICE. *(Overlapping.)* It was Nadja.

>   *(Beat.)*

JUNE. Nadja...

>   *(Processing.)*

> The *book* lady?

>   *(Beat.)*

> Are you *fuckin* her too?

ALICE. WHAT?

JUNE. Are you?

ALICE. Seriously?

JUNE. *Come with you to Atlanta?* I think maybe you need to call your sponsor, I think maybe you missed a step. Aren't you supposed to go buy a ficus or somethin, a plant, make sure it doesn't die, ya know, from hoverin?

>   *(**BIB** begins to gasp for breath. **WEEZY** cries out again.)*

(Intermittent goat cries (of pain, fear, sadness, etc.) from both **BIB** *and* **WEEZY** *throughout the remainder of the scene. Their cries – indeed, the throes of death – ebb and flow as a counterpoint to* **ALICE** *and* **JUNE***'s heated exchange. We should be able to hear all the dialogue clearly.)*

*(***ALICE** *retrieves another cup of kibble.)*

ALICE. OK, first of all, she's engaged. And second of all, to a MAN. And third of all, not in SIX lifetimes, OK, Nadja's like a mother to me, not that I need to defend this – ya know this is bullshit.

JUNE.	ALICE.
(Overlapping.) I'm not jealous, Alice, don't care.	*(Pouring kibble out the window.)* I'm feeding your goats, June, I'm feeding your goats!

JUNE. Do what you want. I'm stupid anyway, why are you even here? Just go.

ALICE.	WEEZY & BIB.
OK, there, that, that right there, that's what I'm talking about, those words, they're all mixed up and crazy and I can't fight that, that's like how a child talks, and you're not a child, you're a grown woman. You have to know what you want, June.	*(Intermittent goat cries.)* *(Intermittent goat cries.)* *(Intermittent goat cries.)*

    (Beat.)

What do you want?!

JUNE. I DON'T KNOW!

    (The goat cries intensify for a moment.)

ALICE.   **WEEZY & BIB.**

> *(To the* **GOATS***.)* Do you mind? We are in *CRISIS*!

> *(To* **JUNE***.)* You are holding on to an illusion. Some...some idea of wholeness, something that you created in your own head, June, and it served you once, but not

> anymore. You can choose. You can actually do that. You can decide that you've done enough and you can walk out that door.

> *(Intermittent goat cries.)*

> *(Intermittent goat cries.)*

> *(Intermittent goat cries.)*

WEEZY. *(To* **BIB***.)* It's OK, Mama.

JUNE.   **ALICE.**

> I tell you what, I'll walk out that door the day you pick up that phone call from your dad.

> Easy peasy. Right?

>   You can't compare that, it's not the –

JUNE. I think I just did. *Not the same?* Not the *second-hardest-thing* you / can imagine?

ALICE. *(Overlapping.)* We're talking about *you,* June.

JUNE. Right.

ALICE. You brought me here for a reason. Remember that part? Do you?

JUNE. Just go.

ALICE. You have to leave this place!

JUNE. Get the fuck outta here!

JUNE.   **ALICE.**

> *(A yelp.)* NOBODY WANTS THIS!

>   Nope.

(**ALICE** *retrieves her cell phone, opens up a photo gallery and hands the phone to* **JUNE**.)

JUNE. What?

ALICE. Scroll.

JUNE. Scroll.

ALICE. Just swipe.

JUNE. *Swipe.* What the fuck is swipe?

> (**JUNE** *swipes the whole phone back and forth in the air like a windshield wiper. This has the adorable effect of bringing the whole argument to a screeching halt.*)

ALICE. Watch – stop – that's fucking adorable, here, let me show you.

JUNE.	**ALICE**.
I'm so dumb.	
Ugh, this is torture.	Take one finger.

ALICE. That way. Scroll that way.

JUNE. *(Regarding the photo on the phone.)* That's Weezy. How'd you get in there, Weezy?

ALICE. *(Overlapping – correcting.)* Other way.

JUNE.	**ALICE**.
You see my swipin?!	The *other* way.

ALICE. No the *other* other way.

JUNE. *(Frustrated.)* Ohmahgod, would you make up your –

> (**JUNE** *draws a quick breath, reacting to the photograph on her screen. Projection: The photographs, candid photos taken of* **JUNE** *when she was outside playing with* **WEEZY** *and* **BIB**, *come to life around the room.*)

ALICE. That's *you*. That's what I see. You look at me and tell me she's not beautiful. Tell me. You can't because you know I'm right. You can keep scrolling, there's more.

(Beat.)

She's not sad, June. NOT SAD.

> *(Silence.)*

> *(**JUNE** scrolls through the photographs. Her reaction to the photographs is varied and profound, but she does what she can to contain her emotions.)*

> *(**JUNE** turns slowly on **ALICE**, almost menacing...)*

JUNE. *(Ice cold.)* Did *any* part of you think maybe for *one second* I might not be ready to see this?

ALICE. *(Hesitant.)* I dunno, I thought maybe if you could / see the –

JUNE. *(Overlapping.)* Don't think, don't think. Here's a thing about death Alice. S'triggers everywhere. That's why we *talk* to / each other. We *communicate.*

ALICE.	**JUNE.**
You don't have a lock on death June.	*(Continuous.)* So we don't *hurt* each other just casually walking around on two feet and what-not.

ALICE. *(Overlapping – sarcastic.)* How could I have / known that, June? You're a fucking BRAT, ya know that? Grow up!

JUNE. *(Overlapping.)* Seriously, you hand me your fuckin phone like that, are you cracked? Your girl and your baby are just barely gone and you're comin after me? This is sick! All of it! You're not over them. And guess what, you won't ever be, because those motherfuckers, they take a part of you and LEAVE and they don't come back. There is no "wholeness," Alice. It's just an ache. And it's endless. So, *thank you so much, Alice,* I really appreciate you tryin and all, but don't come in here bringin your pain to *(Making air quotes.)* "_mix in with mine._" I really – *REALLY* – wish you wouldn't!

*(**JUNE** exits.)*

ALICE. *(Calling.)* Question...

JUNE. *(Calling from off.)* No!

ALICE. *(Calling.)* QUESTION!!!

> *(Long pause.)*

> *(**JUNE** re-enters.)*

> *(Pause.)*

JUNE. *(Softly.)* Go...

ALICE. *(Calm and collected.)* Am I not feeling bad enough for you? Is that what this is?

> *(Beat.)*

When you and your...*cousin*...were *looking through my pictures*, and...digging into my personal life, just so I know, what / else did you find?

JUNE. That's not / what that was.

ALICE. BE QUIET!!! I'm talking now.

> *(Beat.)*

Page Six? Oh, that was fun. Picture me: Monday rush, Varick and Watts, passed out next to a maggot-filled dumpster. You found that one, right, when you were doing all of your..."research"? Couch-surfing in Bushwick? Coke at The Roxy? Oh, oh, what was it? There was a *thing* when I drove my dad's Porsche [I think.] off an overpass up in Pearl River.

> *(**WEEZY**'s cries intensify now, and escalate through the remainder of the scene...)*

But I see it now, June, I do. There's an order, a process. If I had only just done the hard work and locked myself away for *three years* with a

> *(Pointing toward the goat noises.)*

TALKING GOAT and another one *DYING*, just *think* what I could have been.

> *(Beat.)*

I am so glad I met you, June. I am SO HAPPY I'm here, and by the way...

(**WEEZY**'s *world cracks open.*)

(Continuous.) <u>FUCK. YOU</u>!!!! Fuck you, June!

WEEZY. *(Softly.)* Mama?

ALICE.	WEEZY.
<u>YOU DON'T GET TO BE THE ONLY ONE</u>!	MAMA?! MAMA?!

WEEZY. *(Continuous.)* MAMAAAAAAAAAAAAAAA!!!!!

JUNE. *(Overlapping. Racing out the door.)* I'm comin Weezy!

WEEZY. *(Softly. Almost childlike.)* Mama... mamaaaaa... mama...

Requiem

(Part dream. Part not. A blanket of moonlight. Delicate music*. A calm.)

*(***WEEZY*** *and* ***BIB****, as before.* ***WEEZY*** *holds a lifeless* ***BIB*** *in her arms.)*

*(***BIB*** *slowly opens her eyes and sits up. She stands up tall. She is strong and able as if in her prime. She removes all of her garments except for a white cotton slip and hands them in a bundle to* ***WEEZY****. She comforts* ***WEEZY*** *with a kiss on the forehead.)*

(Projection (optional): a baby goat, playing.)

*(***BIB*** *looks around the yard for a moment. She finds a garden that looks right enough for a grave and kneels in front of it. She gathers the dark earth in her hands and piles it into a mound. She clutches two handfuls of soil to her chest and closes her eyes to pray. She allows her body to release all of the pain. The emotions come. She allows them for as long as is necessary to be done with the living world. She inhales. She opens her eyes.)*

BIB. *(Joyfully.)* Amen...

*(***BIB*** *covers the grave with dark earth. She stands. She looks back at the house, at* ***WEEZY*** *in a trance, still clutching her garments.)*

WEEZY. Amen...

*(***WEEZY*** *exits.)*

---

* A license to produce *Alabaster* does not include a performance license for any third-party or copyrighted music. Licensees should create an original composition or use music in the public domain. For further information, please see Music Use Note on page 3.

(**JUNE** *enters the grave site area with a basket of pine cones and flowers.*)

(**BIB** *approaches* **JUNE***, smiling. She blows a gentle puff of air into* **JUNE***'s hair and then exits.*)

Scene Two

(As before.)

*(**JUNE** approaches **BIB**'s grave. **WEEZY** looks out at the horizon. They are both raw with emotion now.)*

*(**JUNE** places flower petals and pine cones on **BIB**'s grave.)*

JUNE. She was so good.

(Beat.)

I'm sorry Weezy.

WEEZY. *(Numb.)* You have to leave this place.

JUNE. Well, I'll just waltz right on out then.

WEEZY. Waltz, walk, / whatever.

JUNE. *(Overlapping.)* Until I die. With no oxygen / until I'm asphyxiated.

WEEZY. *(Overlapping.)* Good God, so dramatic.

JUNE. *(Overlapping.)* Until I'm – dyin is dramatic, yes, dyin is dramatic!

WEEZY. Mama died easy, Mama wasn't dramatic, she died in her fuckin sleep.

JUNE. OK, Bib is a *goat*!

WEEZY. *(Stung.)* That's right, June, Bib is a *goat*.

JUNE.	**WEEZY**.
I'm not a goat!	*You're* not a goat!!!

WEEZY. What are you waitin for, anyway, *blueprints*?

JUNE. You're not angry at me, you're angry at the world.

WEEZY. How the hell would you know?

JUNE. You can't hurt me.

WEEZY. Outstanding.

JUNE. *(Softening.)* Weezy.

WEEZY. *(A yelp.)* EVERYTHING DIES HERE!

(Pause.)

(**WEEZY** *has one last difficult task to take care of. She is emotional but pushes through and gets down to business.*)

When you sit down with a new piece of wood, you have it all planned out, or no?

JUNE. No.

WEEZY. No?

JUNE. No.

WEEZY. So, how does it work?

JUNE. I just...begin, I guess, I get your point, I do.

WEEZY. You have to want it, do you want it?

(**JUNE** *nods.*)

OK then. Tell me what you want. What you dream about.

JUNE. Naps?

WEEZY. June.

JUNE. A day without pain?

WEEZY. Close your eyes.

JUNE. I don't –

WEEZY. Close.

JUNE. What –

(**JUNE** *closes her eyes.* **WEEZY** *breathes,* **JUNE** *breathes with her.*)

WEEZY. Just tell me what you see.

JUNE. See where?

WEEZY. (*About to lose it.*) Make. Shit. Up.

(*Pause.* **JUNE** *tries to "see"...*)

JUNE. (*Unsure where to begin.*) What am I –

WEEZY. OK, start with the ridge line.

JUNE. The ridge line.

WEEZY. (*Firmly – at the breaking point.*) The one in front of our *house.*

(**JUNE** *and* **WEEZY** *stand side by side, both facing the ridge line.*)

JUNE. Oh, the ridge line.

WEEZY. Got it?

JUNE. Yeah.

WEEZY. You see the old lean-to in the South Forty?

JUNE. Yeah.

WEEZY. Good.

JUNE. I gotta trash that lean-to.

WEEZY. Ya can't, there's kittens.

JUNE. Kittens?!

WEEZY. Brand new litter o' kittens, under that lean-to.

JUNE. Are you shittin me?

WEEZY. Look down there.

JUNE. *("Seeing" the kittens.)* I see'em! Oh...it's that one-eyed barn cat from McCray's.

WEEZY. S'right.

JUNE. How sweet.

WEEZY. Now look around, what else y'see?

JUNE. Umm. That dried creek bed.

WEEZY. Yeah?

JUNE. The markers.

WEEZY. What else?

> *(Beat.)*

JUNE. *(Stunned.)* I see Amy.

WEEZY. Is she happy?

> *(Pause.)*

JUNE. *(Taking it in – overwhelmed.)* She is...

WEEZY. Good. Good. Keep walkin.

> *(**JUNE** keeps "walking." Something unnerves her.)*

JUNE. It's black.

WEEZY. Don't stop here.

JUNE. God.

WEEZY. Keep. Walkin.

JUNE. I can't. It's blocked.

WEEZY. Push.

JUNE. It's blocked!

WEEZY. PUSH!!!

> *(Pause.)*

JUNE. OK...

WEEZY. Got it?

JUNE. It's clearin.

WEEZY. Yeah?

JUNE. *(Nodding.)* It's clearin.

> *(Beat.)*

It's...there's a light.

WEEZY. A light?

JUNE. *(An awakening.)* I can see the pasture...

WEEZY. Keep walkin.

JUNE. OK.

WEEZY. Now what?

JUNE. The meadow...

WEEZY. Look all around.

JUNE. *(Part enthralled, part awkward.)* I don't know what I'm doin!

WEEZY. Imagine the most beautiful thing.

JUNE. The most – OK, like what?

WEEZY. Whatever you want.

JUNE. *(Agitated.)* I'm supposed to imagine somethin I've never imagined before?

WEEZY. Do it.

JUNE. I –

> *(**WEEZY** reaches for **JUNE**'s hand. They are now side by side, hand in hand, looking out at "the picture" **JUNE** is "painting" in her imagination. **JUNE** settles.)*

WEEZY. *(Tenderly.)* Put yourself in a picture.

JUNE. A picture? I –

(Pause.)

(Digging in now.)

I'm walkin.

WEEZY. *(Sweetly.)* Good, good, where?

JUNE. *(Somewhat urgently.)* I don't know, a *road* somewhere. It's mornin, early mornin, and there's fog but it's liftin. There's a field on the right. With horses, Appaloosa.

WEEZY. Are you still walkin?

JUNE. I'm walkin. The pavement is black as pitch and the stripin is new. I don't know this road, it's some road, somewhere not in Alabama.

WEEZY. How do you know?

JUNE. I feel it. It's far. It's far away.

> (**WEEZY** *is visibly moved. As* **JUNE** *gains momentum,* **WEEZY** *slowly falls apart.)*

WEEZY. *(Emotional.)* Is it beautiful?

JUNE. *(Profoundly moved.)* Oh...yes. It is.

WEEZY. How?

JUNE. It's...it's open. It's *wide* open...there's...mountains maybe, faint purple mountains. And a crevasse. Like where a glacier used to hang. I'm in a watercolor. Wow...

(Pause.)

Now there's a car. It's comin toward me.

WEEZY. What color?

JUNE. I can't – yellow. Bright yellow, like from another paintin.

(Amused.)

I'm in another paintin, no, I'm in the same paintin.

WEEZY. *(Mostly to herself.)* You're laughin.

JUNE. Oh, my God, it's Bennie Heartsill from third grade and she's drivin a car, but she's still in third grade, how · is she drivin a car?

(More laughter from **JUNE**.*)*

Oh, she's pullin over. She's almost crashed. She cannot drive that car. Oh, I see now, she's sittin on a pile of encyclopedias! She looks exactly the same, except her hair is *crimson red.*

(Pause.)

WEEZY. *(To the audience.)* It's not *not* love to walk away.

JUNE. What on Earth is she doin here?

WEEZY. *(To the audience.)* Hate me if you need to. I need nothin but a sense of good direction.

JUNE. She's pullin me into the car now, she's laughin.

WEEZY. *(To the audience – pointedly.)* I leave everything I gave. And that's *a lot.*

JUNE. Wow...she hasn't changed a bit.

> (**WEEZY** *releases* **JUNE**'s *hand, kisses her matter-of-factly on the forehead and exits with a quickness.)*

> (**JUNE** *reacts to the sudden absence of* **WEEZY**. *She reaches into the void for* **WEEZY**'s *hand but she knows now that* **WEEZY** *is gone for good. She is distraught but she tries desperately to stay on task.)*

(Faltering.) We're...we're in this old beat up yellow convertible. Five-speed.

(Gaining strength now...pushing through.)

The top is down and there's music. On the *radio.*

(As if transported by angels...)

We're off now and we're drivin.
Drivin. Fast.

(A sharp inhale – as if seeing the face of God...)

Into the sun!

Scene Three

(A few hours later.)

*(**ALICE** enters **JUNE**'s bedroom carrying items from a shopping trip. She sets them down and sits on the edge of the bed, bags packed. **JUNE** enters and stands in the doorway. The following exchange occurs with **ALICE**'s back to **JUNE**.)*

ALICE. This is nothing like *Bridges of Madison County*.

> *(Beat.)*

It's not.

JUNE. How? How is it not? Farm girl, photographer, one hot weekend and now you're at the light with your blinker on and I'm back here in your rear-view mirror.

ALICE. You can't do *Bridges*. And that's an awfully convenient comparison. I asked you to come with me.

JUNE. *(Proving her point.)* Clint Eastwood.

ALICE. OK, first of all, you're not married. Or are you? Are you a Polish housewife?

JUNE. Polish?

ALICE. Meryl Streep.

JUNE. She wasn't Polish she was Italian*.

ALICE. What?

JUNE. She was Italian.

> *(Now turning to look at **JUNE**.)*

ALICE. I thought she was Polish.

JUNE. She always sounds Polish.

ALICE. Who does?

JUNE. Meryl Streep!

ALICE. *(Thinking.)* Oh, oh, yeah, she does.

> *(Moving on. Begin rapid fire.)*

---

* Pronounced: EYE-tal-yun.

(Words tumbling.) OK, not married. Not a lonely *Polish-EYE-tal-yun-American* house wife. Meryl Streep had the whole thing, OK, the husband, the kids, all that shit, she had too much to lose. And furthermore, it's not raining.

JUNE. What? Oh, not / rainin, not rainin.

ALICE. *(Overlapping.)* In the movie, on the day he drove away from her. / *Not raining,* June.

JUNE. *(Overlapping.)* OK, *that* was a directorial decision, and therefore, I don't think you're allowed to count that one, Alice. Otherwise and aside from the downpour, it's just like *Bridges of Madison County.*

> *(End rapid fire. Pause.)*

ALICE. I don't know what it is…

> *(Beat.)*

JUNE. You have feelins for me?

> *(Beat.)*

What kind of feelins?

ALICE. The scary kind?

JUNE. I see.

> *(**ALICE** takes a deep breath.)*

ALICE. OK, two things. The first one's hard.

JUNE. Well don't drag it out, just say it.

ALICE.	**JUNE.**
I am, would you – Shhhhhhhut-it…	Quick, like a band-aid.

> *(**JUNE** settles.)*

ALICE. It goes like this. I selfishly wish that you would come with me for reasons that may or may not be *smart* or *healthy* or *ethical* even. OK? So that's out loud. Was that out loud?

JUNE. Sooo out loud.

ALICE. Great. *And. Also.* Atlanta. Birmingham. I'll drop you off at a damn Texaco, *wherever.* It's just really *really* important, June, that you not do *this* anymore.

> *(Pause.)*

What do you have to lose, exactly? A day, a few nights in really cool city? What does that cost you?

> (**ALICE** *retrieves the travel books from the shelf.*)

Pick one.

> (**JUNE** *takes the travel books from* **ALICE** *and throws them across the room.*)

> *(Beat.)*

(A half joke.) It's a good start.

> *(Pause.)*

You do understand what this is, right? If I leave here without you, you die.

JUNE. WhatEVER.

ALICE. And that's not an exaggeration, you've got one foot in the grave already. The barn is gone, June.
(Referring to the piles of wood.) This is not a barn anymore, it's a coffin. I can't leave you here to rot away and / bury yourself, I won't do it.

JUNE. *(Overlapping.) These are the days of our lives...*

ALICE. Everything is a joke to you.

JUNE. No, just the shit you / say.

ALICE. *(Overlapping.)* You're hard to love, ya know that?

> *(Beat.)*

We get in my rental, we drive away from here together. A hundred and forty miles. It's a start. And if you don't like it, you can take a cab right home, OK? That's a good deal. You should really take it.

> (**ALICE** *retrieves the gold cross necklace and hands it to* **JUNE**.)

JUNE. Mama's cross. Where was this?

ALICE. Out back, in the grass.

> (**JUNE** *takes a moment to touch the object and warm it with her hands. She puts the necklace on.*)

JUNE. *(Heartfelt.)* Thank you.

> *(Pause.)*

I need to apologize for somethin. That stuff I said about you *comin on to me,* or whatever, it was wrong for me to say that, for a lotta reasons, yes, I was angry and yes, I was tryin to hurt you but that's not even it. What you're doin is *important.* What you're doin with these women is really, *really necessary* and I'm not even talkin about the photographs, I mean yes, they're beautiful and you *exalt* these women and I think that that's *amazin* but it's somethin else, Alice, I've been thinkin about it and I figured it out. You have this thing in you, this *gift*. It's how you see people, Alice. I don't know how you do it, but it's amazin. And this thing now with these women...and the way that you come to where we are and you see "it" and you see us and you see how broken we are and you see the beauty instead and you tell us that we're beautiful and not for one second did I think I was beautiful, in my whole life nobody ever said I was beautiful, but you did and I won't ever be the same after that. And I don't want to make this about me, this is so much bigger than me, and this is nothin like *Bridges of Madison County,* although it kind of is but not really – I don't expect to run away with you, I know that's not what this is – I just... I want you to know how *grateful* I am.

> *(Beat.)*

I'm so grateful...

> *(Pause.)*

ALICE. I want you to give me your hand and walk with me out of this house.

JUNE. So easy.

ALICE. No...

JUNE. What am I supposed to do in Atlanta while you're takin pictures? Is there a giant ball of twine or somethin'?

ALICE. Atlanta doesn't give a shit.

> (**ALICE** *pulls out a travel-sized art kit that she purchased for* **JUNE** *and hands it to her.*)

JUNE. *(Reading the label.) Travel size.*

ALICE. I got maps, I got this weird – it's like a third grade atlas... *probably* – and I got you six of these...

> (*She hands her a handful of art journals.*)

for sketches. I bought every one they had. You're not going to believe this but that's the first time I've ever been inside a Wal-Mart.

> (*Beat.*)

It was pretty much like Christmas. Adderall Christmas.

> (**JUNE** *looks down at the kit again. She opens it and a little trinket falls out. She retrieves it.*)

Oh, that's from a gum ball machine. It's a baby elephant. For luck.

> (**JUNE** *returns the baby elephant to the travel kit and touches a few of the contents with her fingers. She is overcome.*)

> (**JUNE** *walks over to* **ALICE**. *She pauses. She touches* **ALICE**'*s hair.*)

> (*She touches* **ALICE**'*s face, tracing the details of her skin as if committing them to memory. She kisses* **ALICE** *tenderly on the lips.* **ALICE** *kisses her back. They release.*)

> (**JUNE** *hands the travel kit back to* **ALICE**.*)

JUNE. Be safe.

(**JUNE** *exits.*)

(**ALICE** *sets the travel kit and journals on the night stand. She notices the newly-completed painting: two figures, wrapped in an embrace.* **ALICE** *becomes emotional and has a quiet moment to herself before leaving a note on* **JUNE***'s pillow. She gathers up her bags to walk out. Just as* **ALICE** *turns to leave,* **JUNE** *enters the room wearing a colorful windbreaker and carrying a suitcase.*)

(*Beat.*)

I'm back.

(*Beat.*)

ALICE. (*Amused.*) You're giving me a suitcase?

JUNE. (*Nervously.*) Did you need one?

This one has a mouth wash...like a *Listerine* stain...in the inside pocket – Atlanta doesn't give a shit.

ALICE. I've never been to Atlanta.

(*Beat.*)

JUNE. It's big.

ALICE. I've heard.

(**ALICE** *demonstrates the calming breath.* **JUNE** *inhales through her nose and out through her mouth. They inhale – .*)

(*Interrupting cellphone:* **ALICE***'s cell rings with the same VERY UNPLEASANT RINGTONE.* **ALICE** *lets it ring twice.*)

JUNE. Second hardest thing you'll ever do.

ALICE. I can't.

JUNE. You can.

(*Beat.*)

You *can*.

(*The phone continues to ring.*)

(**ALICE** *takes a deep breath and answers the phone.*)

ALICE. *(As she answers the phone – to* **JUNE**.*)* I hate you. *(To the caller.)* Hello?

(*Long pause.*)

Hi, Dad.

(*Beat.*)

I'm not crying, *you're* crying.

(*Lights fade.*)

End of Play

National New Play Network
Rolling World Premiere

NATIONAL NEW PLAY NETWORK

National New Play Network is an alliance of professional theaters that work together in innovative ways to develop, produce, and extend the life of new plays. NNPN's flagship initiative, the Rolling World Premiere (RWP) program, supports three or more Member Theaters that choose to fully mount the same new play within eighteen months, agreeing to share the World Premiere designation amongst them. This allows the playwright to develop their new work with distinct creative teams in multiple communities, making adjustments based on what is learned from each production's artists and audiences.

To date, NNPN has championed the RWPs of more than ninety new plays that have gone on to receive hundreds of subsequent productions across the US and around the world, been nominated for and/or won the Pulitzer Prize, Steinberg/ATCA, Stavis, PEN, and Blackburn awards, and adapted into feature films. The playwrights supported by the RWP program are emerging, established, and renowned artists, many of whom credit an NNPN RWP as a major step in their career. Learn more about NNPN and RWPs at www.nnpn.org.